BRUTAL

BRUTAL

Michael Harmon

ALFRED A. KNOPF

NEW YORK

THIS IS A BORZOI BOOK PUBLISHED BY ALFRED A. KNOPF

Published in the United States by Alfred A. Knopf, an imprint of Random House Children's Books, a division of Random House, Inc., New York.

Visit us on the Web! www.randomhouse.com/teens

Educators and librarians, for a variety of teaching tools, visit us at www.randomhouse.com/teachers

Library of Congress Cataloging-in-Publication Data
Harmon, Michael B.
Brutal / Michael Harmon. —1st ed.
p.   cm.
Summary: Forced to leave Los Angeles for life in a quiet California wine town with a father she has never known, rebellious sixteen-year-old Poe Holly rails against a high school system that allows elite students special privileges and tolerates bullying of those who are different.
ISBN 978-0-375-84099-9 (trade) — ISBN 978-0-375-94099-6 (lib. bdg.)
[1. High schools—Fiction. 2. Schools—Fiction. 3. Social isolation—Fiction.
4. Bullies—Fiction. 5. Fathers and daughters—Fiction. 6. Mothers and
daughters—Fiction. 7. Singers—Fiction. 8. Moving, Household—Fiction.
9. California—Fiction.] I. Title.
PZ7.H22723Bru2009
[Fic]—dc22
2008004718

The text of this book is set in 12-point Celeste.

Printed in the United States of America
March 2009
10 9 8 7 6 5 4 3 2 1
First Edition

For

Sydney and Dylan

This novel was written for all teenagers out there who have the courage to stand up for something they believe to be true, and the willingness to overcome mistakes made in trying to make a difference in this world. It's also for the parents, teachers, and administrators who listen to them.

Chapter One

If I'd known I'd be living in Benders Hollow, California, when I was sixteen, I would have traded back every complaint I had about my life for a bus ticket out of this place. No can do, though. I'm stuck here for a year. Then I'll be gone, back to Los Angeles and on my own.

I met Benders Hollow four minutes ago via a Greyhound bus because my mom, Dr. Nancy M. Holly, decided her "path" didn't include being a mom anymore. As I stepped on the bus to come here, she stepped on a private chartered jet, headed to some South American jungle village to help "world citizens" lance boils and disinfect festering monkey bites. All so she could come back and tell her doctor friends how she helped the underprivileged peons she looks down her long nose at.

Not that I'm complaining. At this point I don't care if I see her until I get a monkey bite. I get in the way of her life, and we're like gunpowder and lightning together. First it was two weeks in Syria helping refugees. She missed my seventh-grade graduation for that one. Then it was a month in Africa. Scratch my fifteenth birthday for that trip, but add a purple Mohawk to greet her when she got back. Sometimes spite tastes sweet, and she refused to take me to any of her "functions" because it's not who you are, it's what you look like, and until I looked normal, I was out of the loop. Damn, no more jumbo shrimp cocktail and old pervert doctors ogling my ass.

Now it's a year in South America. I don't even know what country. I didn't ask.

Not that her being gone is much different from her being here, because even when she's here, she's gone. Whatever. My mom is saving the world one person at a time, she likes to say. I like to ask her how it feels to think you're a god. She rolls her eyes and walks away.

I'm in a no-win situation, though, and I know it. Poor disaffected me. We're rich. I've been quietly "transferred" out of three high-end private schools due to my inability to follow stupid rules. My last school counselor asked me how I could possibly complain about having such a great life and wonderful mother. Yeah, everybody loves her, and she loves everybody loving her. For such a stupid and lame question, I started crying before I got pissed about it. My mom cares more about strangers than about me.

She saves lives and that's good, and I love her because she's not always as selfish and egotistical as it seems, but it ends with the one thing more important than her status. Money. I asked her how many families she put through bankruptcy while she was saving their lives and she didn't speak to me for a week.

Anyway, now she's working as a surgeon in remote parts of a jungle where her daughter isn't, and I'm in Benders Hollow to meet my father for the first time because she wouldn't let me stay home alone. It's not like I haven't taken care of myself since I was ten, and it's not like he has. I can order out. I know how to use a toaster. Big deal. No different from when she's in town.

My mom likes telling me I'm spoiled. I'm a rich kid stuck in a not-rich-kid mind. She says I am who I am because I'm reactionary to her perfectness. But I'm not. I fit nowhere in her life, and the embarrassment I see in her face and the way she falters and casts her eyes away when she introduces me to "colleagues" makes me want to vomit on her four-hundred-dollar shoes. But I know who I am. I'm Poe Holly, and I'm pissed off.

"Poe?"

I recognized him from a picture I saw once, but more than that, I recognized his voice. I'd talked to him a few times before. Once at Christmas when I was ten, another time on my birthday, and then after I'd been caught drinking last year in the locker room of my last private school. My mother's daughter doesn't get suspended. It was decided Oak Grove Preparatory School was not good enough for me.

I saw the resemblance in his eyes. The color of flagstone, just like mine. Other than that, he was totally and completely average. He could be any Joe Schmoe walking down the street in a small town: slim build, beige jeans, and a tucked-in slate green short-sleeved polo shirt. Every woman's dream if her dream was bland: he was about as clean-cut and boring as you could be. The only thing cool about him was that he wasn't wearing an article of clothing worth over fifty dollars. Maybe we'd get along.

His hair was cut ultra-conservative, dark brown like

mine if I didn't dye it black, and he was clean-shaven and looked older than I had imagined. I knew he was thirty-five, but his face was a bit drawn and the shade under his eyes reminded me of a person who read too much. He smiled, standing with his hands in his pockets. I could tell he was nervous. I stepped toward him. "Hi."

He nodded, shifting his feet. "Hello."

We stood there, me in my punk getup and him looking completely forgettable with his loafers and neatly parted hair. I hitched my bag on my shoulder, wondering if this had been a good idea. "You're not holding a sign."

He blinked, then furrowed his brow.

"A sign. Like at an airport. It's supposed to say my name. Poe Holly. So I don't miss you in the crowd."

He brightened, then smiled, looking around the vacant sidewalk. "Nobody else got off at this stop."

"I was the only one *on* the bus. I take it the usual tourists don't come by Greyhound."

He laughed. "Benders Hollow isn't Los Angeles, and no, they don't."

I looked around, taking in the touristy setting. Mom had offered to have a limo bring me up. "Seven hours on a bus?" she'd said. "Poe . . ." Blah blah blah. I sighed. "Well, I'm here."

He held his hand out. "Let me take your bag." He took it, then looked to the bus idling at the curb. "Any more baggage?"

"Mom wouldn't fit in a suitcase."

He smiled, but a darkness passed through his eyes. Then he slung the huge thing over his back and we walked down the street. "That's why I like it."

"Like what?"

"Benders Hollow."

I looked around. It looked like a small town to me, all right. "Why?"

He chuckled, but barely loud enough to hear. "Because it's not Los Angeles."

. . .

We reached his car, a late-model maroon Volvo, and the first thing that struck me was what wasn't in it. Not a dust particle on the dash, a smudge on a window, or an errant leaf on the floor. No papers, wrappers, coffee cups, or trinkets. No change in the tray. Immaculate. Just like my mother. I groaned.

We drove through a few blocks of gift and wine shops with old-fashioned lampposts studding the strip and pruned trees lining the way, with banners celebrating a wine festival fluttering in the breeze. I sighed. The streets were just like my dad. Pristine. No dirty windows, garbage, grime, homeless people, or pollution. There weren't even leaves in the gutters. The place was so sterile I was afraid to breathe.

Past the shopping area, he took a quick right down a street called Mulberry Lane. Maple trees lined the road, and the houses were big and old and nice. There's money here, and it showed. Before I left, I asked Mom what it was like, and she told me she'd never been here, so she couldn't say. She refused to say any more, other than it fit my father to a tee. She was right. He fit Benders Hollow like a surgical glove, and I wondered for a moment why they hadn't stayed together.

Five houses down Mulberry Lane, he turned into a driveway and my assumption was that this was home.

Unless he occasionally parked in other people's driveways. Great. I lived on Mulberry Lane. Next thing I knew, I'd be wearing pigtails and skipping rope down the sidewalk. The house was nice, though, with peaked roofs and a big porch up front shaded with an awning, perfect paint, green trimmed lawn, and a doorbell, which, surprisingly, had a tiny note attached to it. *Out of order. Please knock.*

The whole town reminded me of a *Saturday Evening Post* picture. American culture at its best as long as you didn't turn the page or look deeper than the last brush-stroke. Wine sniffers. Ugh. I'd traded one pretentious hell-hole for another, but unlike back home, there were no raves, concerts, noise, or friends. We sat in the car. "What did she say?"

He cut the engine and sat for a moment. I got the feeling he'd enjoyed the silence of our little trip. He stared out the windshield. "About what?"

"Me. I know you guys talked."

"We did, but not much."

"The last time Mom didn't say much was when Dr. Paulson broke her jaw playing racquetball."

He cocked an eye at me.

"Old boyfriend." I smiled. "A match made in heaven. He got his hair cut every two weeks, subscribed to *Golf Digest,* and read the *Wall Street Journal.* An all-around presentable specimen to be seen with her."

Silence.

I shifted in my seat. "That was a joke."

He tapped the steering wheel absently, something going through his head. "I'm afraid I don't know very much of your life, Poe."

"Nervous?"

He sighed. "Yes. I am." He looked at me. "Are you?"

"A tiny bit. And I don't know *anything* about your life, so we're even."

He nodded, then smiled. "Your mother said that you were having a difficult time adjusting to being a teenager."

"I blame things on other people sometimes, too."

I caught a look on his face out of the corner of my eye, but I couldn't tell what it meant. Not a smile. He nodded. "She didn't speak in those terms to me, if that's what you're wondering. She's proud of you."

I let that one slide.

He shook his head, flustered, not knowing what to do. "I didn't want you to come here expecting this to be enemy territory. I don't think ill of her."

I looked out the window at the tidy house. "I know exactly why I'm here."

"Well, I don't, and I'm not going to judge, okay?"

I smiled. "I will for you, then."

He smiled at that one. "Come on, I'll show you inside."

"I think I'll sit outside for a minute."

He exhaled, then nodded. "Sure. Come on in whenever."

The truth was that I wasn't a bit nervous, I was really nervous. I didn't want to go inside. I didn't want to be here. He seemed nice enough, but it was just so strange. Familiar, but not familiar. He was my *dad,* but Poe Holly didn't have a dad. Poe Holly was the outcome of a sperm donor program called Poor Choices and Bad Mistakes. They'd been married, yes, but for how long I didn't know. Mom never talked about it.

Chapter Two

I sat on the steps of the porch wondering what I should call him. His name was David, but he was also my dad and I figured "hey you" wouldn't do, so I decided to avoid calling him anything. He seemed so white-bread. Homogenized and a total conformist, which was so not me it was funny. This whole place already seemed boring, and if anything, it grated against my whole counterculture being like a chain saw cutting cheese.

I'm a singer. Music is my life. From the Ramones to the Sex Pistols to The Doors to modern-day metal and pop punk like Blink-182, I loved any song that held power. I bled guitar riffs and breathed to sing, and more than anything, I missed my band back home, October Rose. My buds. The guys I hung with at Venice Beach and played with in the warehouse next to Chang's deli off the boulevard.

Los Angeles is noisy and full. Traffic and horns and planes and helicopters and millions of people and billions of machines and everything that made me feel comfortable. Back home, we lived in a posh part of LA that was half an hour from Venice, which just happened to be the place Jim Morrison from The Doors lived and wrote his brilliance before dying. Venice was the place you could hang out and be a part of something great.

Now, I looked around this neighborhood and didn't see a thing. Just a bunch of frozen perfect houses with nice lawns and picket fences. A place I didn't, and wouldn't, fit into. I held my breath for half a minute and didn't even hear a bird chirp. I'd be insane in three days.

"You new around here?"

I turned my head and a guy stood at the waist-high fence separating the yards, his bony hands and skinny fingers resting on the white pickets. About my age, he wore a Kenny Chesney T-shirt with the sleeves cut out, half his white rib cage showing through the armholes, a lump of tobacco in his scraggly lip. His camo shorts and ragged Michael Jordan high-tops showed through the slats of the fence.

I looked at his freckled long face and big ears sticking out under a backwards baseball cap and didn't know whether he'd try to shoot and eat me or pickle me in a vat of vinegar first. He looked like one of God's mischievous little angels had a field day in the cast-off section of the human parts bin, and the expectation I'd had of the teenagers around here fitting more into an Abercrombie & Fitch catalog crumbled. The dude looked straight out of a *Dukes of Hazzard* episode, and I expected Boss Hogg to pop out from behind a tree. "No, I've been here for years. You never noticed?"

He scratched his five-haired scraggly chin, then spit a wonderfully gross stream of brown goo into my dad's yard, tipping his chin up as he did so. "You joking?"

"Yes."

"They call me Velveeta."

That got my attention. He drawled like a gunfighter. "Velveeta?"

He smiled, nodding. "Yeah. I like cheese." He paused. "You like cheese?"

I raised my eyes to the pristine blue sky without even a smidgen of smog in it, wondering why this was happening to me and wishing that I could stop existing just for a little while. That I could wake up in my bed back home and Mom would be two hours gone and I'd have everything I was used to. I didn't belong here. Not in this paralyzed Norman Rockwell painting with an oddly put-together trespasser spitting brown goo all over the canvas. I looked at him. "Do I like cheese? Is that some form of a pickup line?"

He screwed his eyes at me and frowned like I was the biggest idiot in the world, then spit another stream of tobacco juice, this one farther than the last. He looked at where it landed for a minute, nodded at his new record, then sighed. "Shit."

"Shit what?"

He looked me up and down, then looked himself up and down, his eyes pausing on his arms as he flexed his pasty freckled spaghetti strings. "I got a girl."

"Cool."

He nodded, then smiled with half his mouth. An obvious mimic of Elvis, but it reminded me more of a stroke victim. "One-woman man standing here. Sorry."

I almost laughed, but he was so serious I couldn't. "Shot down, then."

"So you like cheese?"

"I would guess about as much as the next person."

"You got a favorite kind?"

I didn't know I'd been transported to cheese world, but I could roll with it. "Swiss."

"You like Velveeta cheese?"

"Sure. On nachos maybe."

He smiled, peeling his lips away from buckteeth into a goofy grin. He had the most expressive face I'd ever seen, morphing from one exaggerated freeze-frame to the next. "Good deal." He moved his hand from the fence and waved. "See you round, then. Gotta take a dump the size of Chicago and it ain't waiting for nothing. Turtle's poppin', roast is done, Momma come home 'cuz the prairie dog's barkin'." Then he walked away, leaving me speechless. Sure, everybody dumps, but they usually don't go around announcing it unless they're six years old. As he reached his porch, he looked back. "You got a name?"

I smiled, liking this guy for some odd reason. I could play the cheese game, too. "Gouda. Gouda Provolone."

He furrowed his brow. "You German or something?"

I looked at him. Did nobody in this place know what a joke was? "Yeah."

He nodded, smiling wide. "Well, I'm gonna shit my pants. See ya."

I watched Velveeta walk into his house and took a minute, staring over the neighborhood. Maybe Velveeta was an apparition. Some sort of hallucinogenic reaction from sitting on a Greyhound bus for so long. He couldn't be real. Nobody says this stuff out loud.

I paused at the front door, uncomfortable with just walking in, then decided that I wouldn't knock. He'd agreed that I could come, and he was my dad after all. As I closed the door behind me, the silence of the neighborhood followed me inside.

Two pairs of shoes, one the loafers I recognized and another a pair of leather sandals, sat side by side to the left of the entry. I had a jolt of "my dad is a homosexual and I'm staring at his lover's shoes" paranoia but then remembered he lived alone. They were his sandals, and this was a no-shoes house. God, I thought. What if he was gay? Maybe that was the reason he left my mom. I didn't doubt for a minute that my mom could turn a man gay.

Beyond the Persian rug runner I stood on, the house sprawled out with dark hardwood shiny enough to make it look like ice coated the floor. To the left of the entry were French doors, open, leading to a formal dining room with six chairs. Another rug, dark and rich colors to match the floor, lay centered in the room. To the right of the entryway was a sitting room with dark brown and brass-studded leather sofas and claw-foot chairs facing each other. Bookshelves (not the kind you buy at Target) lined the walls, and brass lamps were set tastefully around the perimeter.

Contrary to my dad having zero sense of clothes fashion, I realized uncomfortably that this house was blue-ribbon material. Just like his car. And yard. And neighborhood. And town. It could be in a magazine displaying the masculine side of perfect interior decorating, and now I was living here.

/ Mom's taste in décor was just like her fashion sense, and her fashion sense was just like her personality. Clean, no-nonsense, utilitarian, and spare. She owned fourteen black dresses, three red ones, eight gazillion pairs of shoes, and six business suits as sharp as her scalpel. The one piece of art, above the mantel in the condo, depicted a single long-stemmed rose in a clear glass vase. Of course it had thorns. That was my mom for you.

This house was middle class, but single-guy-living-alone middle class, which meant upper middle class. My mom had paid thirty-seven thousand dollars for the sofas in the living room. I'd never seen her sit in them. As I glanced around this place, it was immaculate, but it all seemed lived in. Comfortable to a certain extent.

Straight ahead of me was the main hall with a staircase branching off and going up. The hall continued to the kitchen. I peeked in the sitting room to see if my dad was anywhere and saw another set of open doors, these solid wood, leading to a study, a mahogany desk with a laptop sitting on it inside. David sat behind it, intent on the screen.

I walked through the sitting room and he looked up when I came to the door, then closed his computer and smiled. "I see you found your way in."

I nodded. "I met your neighbor."

He brightened. "Victoria? Very quiet woman. Almost antisocial. She has a nephew about your age living with her."

"Not her. The guy. Velveeta."

His smile disappeared. "Yes. He is somewhat new to Benders Hollow, too. Last year."

"He told me he had to take a dump the size of Chicago."

"That would be Andrew."

"That's his name?"

"Yes, but he does go by Velveeta."

I looked around the room. Darkly lit with paneled walls, more bookcases, a leather reading chair off to the side, and a lamp on a mahogany occasional table that matched the desk. I liked it. "This is a nice house."

He stood. "Thank you." He came around the desk. "Here, let me show you your room. I put your bag there if that's okay?"

"Sure." I followed him out and around to the main hall, then up the stairs. He pointed to a room at the end of the hall, explaining that was his room, the next door was a closet, the next my bathroom, and the door at the other end of the hall was my room.

He opened it and I followed him in. He took a breath, clasping his hands. "I hope this will do. There's another bedroom downstairs off the TV room that you're welcome to, but I thought you'd like this because it's bigger."

I looked around. I had a queen-sized pedestal bed with a real headboard, and even if the comforter was flowered and definitely not me, I didn't care. "It's fine. Thanks."

He brightened, then walked farther in. "I took the liberty of a few things like the dresser and computer for your schoolwork but decided it would be best for you to decorate how you saw fit."

I looked to the computer near the window. "You bought me a computer?"

He nodded, excitement in his eyes. "I didn't know what you'd be bringing, but figured a new gadget or two would be a nice housewarming gift for you." He paused, looking at me. "I want you to make yourself comfortable here, Poe. This is your home."

I didn't know what to say because I knew what this

was. The age-old buying-my-acceptance gig. Get her a bunch of crap so she'll stay out of the way and won't cause trouble. But the light in his eyes told me different. He reminded me of a little boy giving a surprise. It sucked, because I wanted to think it was fake. Every time my mom bought me something, it was to get something. Usually forgiveness, but always something. "Thank you."

"As I said, I waited to buy bedding and such until you got here. We can go tomorrow afternoon and find what suits you."

I looked at the hideous comforter. "It's fine. Really."

He smiled. "Honestly, I had no idea what to expect before you arrived."

For the first time in a long time, I felt self-conscious about what I was wearing, and it made me mad. I looked down at my ripped fishnets and black boots. "I suppose you were hoping for a normal person?"

He shook his head. "Not at all. I made no assumptions. A lady friend told me that the biggest mistake a man can make is picking out clothing or bedding for a lady, so I didn't. You'll have to excuse my ignorance."

Now I felt like an idiot for being a jerk. I covered it with a smile. "Tomorrow sounds fine."

He scrunched up his nose, looking at the bed. "Is it that bad? It's been in the closet for years."

I laughed. "Pretty bad. I'm not a flowery kind of girl."

He nodded. "Very well. Tomorrow it is, then. I'll leave you to unpack and get settled. We'll eat dinner at seven?"

I unzipped my bag, glancing at the clock on my bed stand. Five-thirty. "Sure."

Chapter Three

I looked at my bag, then thought better of unpacking and flopped on the bed. Soft heaven. Some things a girl likes, even punker chicks with black fingernail polish and eyebrow rings, and a nice bed is one of them. This thing alone was almost worth coming to Benders Hollow for.

I woke up to knocking on my door. "Poe?"

I looked at the clock. Seven-thirty. Shit. I scrambled off the bed and opened the door, checking my cheek for drool. "Sorry, I was sleeping."

"Long day, yes?"

I nodded.

"Are you hungry?"

I could tell he was irritated from the tension around his mouth. This was great. First day and I already screwed up. "Yeah. I'll be down in a sec."

I came downstairs a few minutes later, and the table was set for two in the formal dining room. Dad rose from his seat until I took mine, then sat down. I looked at the meal. A fresh salad, baked salmon with lemon slices and purple onion, and some kind of pasta I didn't recognize. "Wow. You're a cook?"

He waved it off. "A hobby."

I sighed, feeling rotten for being late. "You didn't have to do this, really. I'm used to TV dinners and soup."

"I enjoy cooking. Most times it's for one, so this is nice."

"Are you mad? You could have come and got me earlier."

He put his napkin in his lap. "I'm afraid I'm not used to anything but my schedule of things. Living alone has a tendency to create intolerance for other people's way of doing things."

"You sound like a counselor or something."

He looked at me. "I am."

I froze. "You are?"

He nodded. "I take it your mother hasn't talked much of me."

"Nothing."

He took a bite, chewed, laid his fork down, and continued. "Yes, I am a counselor. At the school you'll be attending."

My stomach went queasy. "At my school?"

"Yes."

"My counselor? For my grade?"

He nodded. "The high school here is small. Six hundred students. I'm the counselor for all grade levels."

I ate, suddenly finding a great interest in studying my fish. Wonderful. I had a shrink for a dad, and he was going to be with me all day. "When does school start around here?"

"Next week. Tuesday."

"That's like two weeks earlier than back home."

"You're concerned about me being there? As a counselor?"

I kept my eyes on my plate, my anger building. This

was all fitting together now, and I could imagine the phone conversations Mom had had with him. The last thing I wanted to do on my first day was get heavy with him, but I felt suckered. "I don't need counseling."

He cleared his throat. "You're being defensive, Poe, and there's no threat. Really."

I met his eyes. "I'm not screwed up. I'm not here because of me, I'm here because of my mom. No matter what she told you."

"I told you what she talked of, Poe, and it wasn't bad."

I put my napkin on the table. He was full of shit. I knew my mom well enough to know what she said. She'd blamed it all on me just like she blamed every other crappy thing in her life on other people. I stood. "I know my mother, so you might as well stop."

"I know your mother, too."

That stopped me. He'd just opened a door he shouldn't have, and I could feel it building in my gut. I'd been set up. By him and Mom. I could just see her on the phone, using her diplomatic and caring voice. *Oh God, I'm so concerned about her. It's like I don't know her anymore—she's changed so much. With the black outfits and the way she talks negative about everything, I'm at a loss. Hmmm. Maybe you could help her out, David? Get her back on track? I mean, that's what you do, right?* I knew this deal. I wasn't to blame for our retarded mother-daughter relationship. She just didn't want to be a mom anymore, and they'd both played me. I didn't fit into her perfect elitist life just like I didn't fit here eating salmon with a guy I'd never really ever met. The venom bubbled. Nothing was worse than having somebody look at you and knowing what they were thinking.

What made me even angrier was that here I was on the first day with my stranger dad and I was already getting into a fight with him. I was doomed to conflict, but I couldn't help it. I'd spent years thinking about this moment, and those thoughts had never been good. They'd been full of Poe Holly giving her loser dad both barrels before she rode off into the sunset. "Whatever. I'm sure you know her so well because you were around so much?"

"Poe . . ."

"Don't Poe me. I get enough of that shit from her as it is. I didn't come here because I'm screwed up, I came here because she decided to not be my mom anymore. I'm expendable." I stared at him. "Just like I was expendable when you left."

He sat back, taking a deep breath. The counselor had a problem, and he could eat dirt for all I cared. Even though I felt rotten. He took a minute. "What's the solution to this?"

I looked at him. "What?"

He raised his eyebrows. "You think you're alone in this, Poe? That you're the only one dealing with preconceived assumptions about how you're seen? As much as you wonder how I see you, I wonder how you see me. Will you sit down?"

I looked at him again, wondering what his angle was. Then I sat. "I don't need counseling."

He shook his head. "I'm not saying you do. You're saying you don't."

"I know what this is about."

"I'll tell you what I see if you tell me what you see. Deal? No counseling involved, no talk afterward. Just the truth of what we see."

I took a drink. Now we'd see what the "truth" meant to him. "Fine. You go first."

He folded his hands across his stomach, staring at me. "I see a young woman who feels betrayed by her mother, abandoned by her father, and manipulated by her circumstances. I see you love her and will defend her, but I also see that you've distanced yourself from her. I see anger and resentment toward me, and I see you searching for answers that are hard to find. I also see a smart, articulate, and passionate person who feels like she doesn't belong anywhere, least of all in a place like this, and a person who needs to make a statement to the world. I see you've been uprooted from everything you know, but I also see strength. I don't see fear, though I know you must have it." He looked at me. "I also see a person who thinks she doesn't need help from anybody and a person used to taking care of herself. That's what I see."

Whoa. When he said the truth, he meant it. I felt like my entire life had just been dissected, and I wondered if I was that see-through. I took a breath.

"Your turn."

The truth. Crap. He'd called my bluff, and as everything boiled through my head, I got a little bit nervous, then mad. Fine. If he wanted it this way, he'd have it this way. "Okay. When I got off the bus, I saw average. Blah. A guy who lives alone and is lonely. I see you trying to be fake and full of crap to make me feel good about being here. Buying me things and making things perfect and cooking a great dinner to make me feel better about having a dad who didn't have the guts to have anything to do with his daughter's life for sixteen years. I see a guy who didn't give a crap

20

about anything other than himself, and now I know why you two split up. You're both exactly the same." I clenched my teeth, trying to hold back the torrent he'd invited to the table. Tears of rage welled in my eyes even as I saw him flinch. Like I was physically assaulting him. It pissed me off even more. He was weak. "I see a coward and a selfish bastard who agreed to let me live here because maybe helping me will help him to feel better about what a crappy person he's been for my entire life. I see a guy who's worse than all the other guys my mom brought around because you didn't do anything but sit here and hide in your lonely miserable life for whatever stupid reason you have."

• • •

I felt like bawling my head off because I wanted everything I'd said to be wrong. To be false. It would be so nice to sit at this table and pretend that this man was really my dad. That out of the blue, bammo, I had a nice new father. An addition to a wonderful life. But I didn't. The guy sitting across from me hadn't given a crap for sixteen years, and now a fish dinner and a few hot-key counselor words were supposed to fix it. No dice.

I wiped my eyes, not looking at him, but wanting to desperately. I couldn't. "I'm done."

Silence. Then he spoke. "Very well."

I frowned. He should be yelling at me right now for saying those things. He should be telling me none of it was true and that I didn't understand because I was a kid. Just like Mom always did. "So do we sit here like two idiots or something? Give each other big hugs and go back to pretending everything is cool?"

He shook his head.

I looked up, angry again. "Then what?"

He stood, picking up his plate and glass. "I'm going to do the dishes."

Then he was gone, leaving me with the silence of not knowing what was going on in this awkward, uncomfortable place. If I had just said things like that to my mom, she would have spent the next hour and a half drilling it into me why I was crazy and how I was just looking at it all wrong. He just got up and did the dishes. I wondered how they ever got together in the first place, then picked up my own plate. The one thing my mom always said was that I could never let things alone.

He stood at the kitchen sink with his back to me, rinsing plates. The dishwasher stood open next to him. I walked in, setting my stuff on the counter. I put the rinsed plates in the dishwasher. "What just happened?"

He paused, looking out the window into the darkness. "I wasn't ready for that. I'm sorry."

I wasn't used to this. By now, Mom and I would be going back and forth like machine-gun fire. "Are you mad?"

He shook his head. "No."

I put the last dish in the washer. "Maybe I *should* go home. Maybe this just isn't going to work."

"No." He faced me. "Poe, what you just said to me hurt. Terribly. But I know it's the truth for you, and that's something I have to face. I knew in the back of my mind that those feelings would be there, but I wasn't ready for it. Maybe I hid from it. Hoped it wouldn't come out like this. Maybe I did hope you'd be different in that way."

This is the part where I knew I should apologize, but I don't like those parts, and I didn't want to be anybody other than myself. My mother never apologized for a single thing in her life, at least sincerely, and I'd gotten used to it. "Why'd you ask for it, then?"

"Because the opportunity was there and I knew it had to be done. The sooner the better, I suppose."

"So what do we do now?"

"Turn that knob. I already put the soap in."

I looked at him. "What?"

He turned the dishwasher knob to the start cycle. "What I'm saying is that if you're willing, we move on. Not ignore, but move on. Take it step by step and see what happens."

"You want me here?"

"Yes. I do. And it may be partly selfish, but I do. I want to know you. And I do feel as though I've got to make up for lost time. That's unavoidable."

I nodded, nothing coming to mind other than sappy stuff, and this wasn't a soap opera. He was using all the make-everybody-feel-good adult-speak, but at least he was being honest. "Okay." We stood there not knowing what to do next, so I told him I was going to my room.

He nodded, opened his mouth to say something, then closed it. "I'll be in my study if you need me."

Chapter Four

With school starting in two days, we spent the rest of the weekend shopping. I didn't have a thing for school other than a suitcase full of clothes. Dad showed me the town, which still reminded me of a painting, and I met a few of the locals working cash registers and restaurants. It took me all of a day to tell the difference between the tourists and the townies. Rich tourists have a tendency to look different from the people who serve them, even if the people who serve them make good money.

The main avenue of Benders Hollow was full of wine and gift shops, high-end restaurants, and a few clothes stores with nothing in them I liked. Dad told me the locals never shopped the main strip because the prices were high, so we spent most of our time twenty miles down the highway at an outlet mall. People didn't stare at me as often there, either.

We didn't talk much on Sunday, at least not about anything from last night, and I was thankful. I'd been thinking about it, though, and I knew he was right. I did feel alone and bitter and angry about a lot of things, but he was wrong about one thing. I wasn't consumed by it. This was my life, and if there was one thing my mom taught me, it was that I was the only one responsible for making it different.

I did get new bedding, too. Dad also made me pick out an iPod, a docking station, and some cool speakers for my room, which I felt weird about but accepted, telling him I would pay him back. He shrugged it off and said that certain things were necessities in a teenager's life.

Monday night rolled around and I found out something important. My bathroom was big and the walls and floor were real tile, which meant awesome acoustics. I took a half-hour shower, working my voice through note patterns and bars and missing my band big-time. I'd talked to my buds the morning before and hated it because I was depressed for the rest of the day. Milson had come up with a new riff, hotter than hell, he'd laughed, and my insides crumbled. They'd told me I would be back and they'd wait, but I knew it wouldn't happen. A new singer would come along and I'd be history.

When I came downstairs after my shower, Dad wasn't in his study like he'd been every night after dinner. He was puttering around the kitchen scrubbing the grout lines on the counters with a toothbrush. He made my mom look like a slob.

I leaned against the entry and smiled. I wasn't sure, but I was also beginning to think he didn't have a funny bone in his body. He was dry as a bone in a desert. "Most people use those things on their teeth."

He stopped scrubbing, holding it up and looking at it. "They work well for various cleaning jobs."

I shook my head. "Joke."

He smiled, setting it down on the counter. "Sorry. Are you ready for school tomorrow?"

I rolled my eyes. "Blah."

"Don't like school?"

"Not really my gig."

"Why?"

I shrugged. "Not big on social institutions."

He raised his eyebrows. "I hear a philosophy in there somewhere."

"Not really. I'm just not into being a drone."

"How does an interest in school make you a drone?"

"Conformity. I don't need somebody to tell me what I should be." I looked at him, remembering he was part of it. "No offense."

He nodded. "Your mother mentioned your band."

"My ex-band. And yeah, she thought it was cute until I took it seriously; now she just hates it."

"I heard you singing upstairs. You have an amazing voice."

"Not many teen clubs around here, huh?"

"None. There is the school choir. Award winning."

"No thanks."

"Don't like singing choir songs?"

"Actually, I like singing anything. I just don't like group things. Rules and stuff."

"Give it a thought, huh? It might do well for you."

"Is this the counselor talking or the dad talking?"

He furrowed his brow, thinking. Nothing was a simple answer for him. "The dad. I heard your voice. It is beautiful."

Heat flushed my face. "Thanks."

He picked up the toothbrush. "I can give you a lift tomorrow morning if you'd like."

Though I wasn't the type to be concerned about what other people thought, having the school counselor take me to school on my first day was weird. "I'm walking. Thanks, though."

He nodded. "We'll try to get you enrolled in a driver's ed course. Your mother said you didn't get enrolled in time back home."

"If that's the reason she gave, then I'm sure that's the reason."

"Ah. I see."

I nodded. "I have a question."

He smiled. "Go ahead."

"What do you do in your study every night?"

"Write."

"Like what?"

He shrugged. "Well, I'm working on a book. As a matter of fact, I started it the day you arrived."

"You write?"

He nodded. "Yes."

"Published?"

He looked down. "No."

"Wow. That's cool. What's it about?"

He took a breath. "Well, it's about a girl who goes to live with her father."

I narrowed my eyes. "Don't even tell me . . ."

He smiled. "Joke."

I sighed. "I didn't think you had one in you for a while there. What's it really about?"

A guarded look passed over him. "It's a text on youth. A self-help book of sorts."

"Can I read it?"

"I'm only twenty pages into it."

"I don't care. I can read as you go."

He smiled. "I've a feeling you might not like it."

A self-help book for teens that a teenager wouldn't like. Standard procedure. "I'm not that bad, am I?"

He paused. "I'll let you read it if you agree to think about choir. At least check it out. Mrs. Baird, the choir teacher, is a nice woman."

I figured there would be no harm in that. "Deal."

"Good, then. Maybe we can both benefit. But one thing. You have to be honest if you decide to comment on it."

I rolled my eyes. "No problem there. It comes out in uncontrollable spasms anyway."

He smiled. "I've noticed."

Chapter Five

The first day in a new school requires three things. Paper, pencil, and armor. I put my school ID card around my neck, grabbed my bag, and headed to class. If I could handle Oak Grove Preparatory School and the snobs there, I could handle a podunk wine town with a bunch of rich kids in it. They probably had wine-tasting raves in their parents' sitting rooms and ballroom-danced to Mozart until bedtime. Ooh la la.

As I left the house and stepped on the front porch, I looked over and saw Velveeta standing at the exact spot I met him the first time. He had that big and goofy smile on his face and the same baseball cap backwards covering his wiry red hair, but he'd at least changed his clothes. Today's ensemble included an untucked flannel shirt with the sleeves cut off (he must have a thing for no sleeves), a pair of faded jeans, and Vietnam-era combat boots, half laced.

I figured the huge tobacco bulge in his lip was ever present, and before he said anything, he spit a stream. "Hey, Gouda. How's it going?"

I looked at him. "What?"

He smiled. "You speak-o no English-o?"

Then I remembered what I told him my name was. Gouda Provolone. I smiled. A sucker was born every day. "Oh, fine. Sorry."

He pointed to my backpack. "Looks like you're all ready for school, huh?"

"Well, it is the first day."

"Wanna go together? I could show you the way."

I looked down the street. "You walk?"

"That's what my feet are for." He turned away. "I rode my bike last year, but somebody ruined it. Bent the wheels all up."

I looked at him for a second, not sure I wanted to know how it happened. He'd said it like it was just something that happens every once in a while out of thin air. "Sure. Come on." We walked, and after a block or two of silence, I finally gave in. He might be a sucker, but he was nice. "My name is Poe."

"I know."

I looked at him. "Then why'd you call me Gouda?"

"I'll call you anything you want to be called. Don't matter to me."

"Poe is fine."

"Sounds French. You shave your pits?"

I laughed. You couldn't tell what was a joke with this guy. "Yeah. And no, I'm not French."

"So then how'd you get a name like Poe?"

"My mother's favorite poet is Edgar Allan Poe."

"Weird."

"Yeah. A doctor who likes poetry about death."

He laughed. "I shaved mine once. My pits. Got all itchy

and stuff for like a week. Felt like I had a bunch of red ants in 'em. Drove me crazy."

"I'm not even going to ask why you did it."

We turned the corner and he spit again. "I was into heavy lifting. You know, weights. All the bodybuilder guys shave. Makes it so you can see the muscles better."

"Oh. That makes sense."

"Not really. I still lift, though." He held up an arm and flexed. Spaghetti with meatballs.

"Impressive."

"I know I ain't big yet, but I will be. One day."

"Cool. So you came here last year?"

He nodded, staring at the pavement while we walked. "Yep. At the beginning of the school year. My parents got killed in a car crash. Bam. Just like that. Dead."

"Sorry."

He smiled that goofy smile, but the corners of his mouth turned down. "That's what life gives you if you don't watch out. No use complaining about it, I guess. Yer dad said I should grieve more, but I don't see it."

"My dad?"

"You didn't know he's the counselor?"

"Yeah, I do. It's just taking some time to get used to, I guess."

"Everything does. Take time to get used to, I mean."

"You like the school?"

He shrugged. "School is school. This place is different. You'll prob'ly get shit for looking like you do. Everybody looks the same here."

"I noticed."

"Bunch of high-minded people runnin' around, but it's

not that bad. The food is better than back home. You get to pick here. Like a buffet-type thing. You like buffet?"

I hitched my pack further up on my shoulder. "Where are you from?"

"Lucerne Valley."

"Out past Bakersfield in the Mohave Desert?"

"Born and raised."

"Cool. I like the desert."

"Hotter'n shit in the summer, but it's all good. That's where my girl is."

I didn't want to touch that one. "You have your schedule?"

He shook his head. "They give it to you in homeroom. That way all the new kids can look like idiots running around trying to find classes five minutes after they find out where they're supposed to go."

I blinked at that and realized Velveeta was more savvy than he let on. We walked the rest of the way talking about classes and what teachers he liked and didn't like, and I found out that Velveeta was pretty much a good guy if not the biggest dork I'd ever met. He didn't even have a bad thing to say about a teacher who didn't like him, Mr. Reed, his social studies teacher from last year.

There were six hundred students at Benders High, and they were bused from three surrounding communities in the area—other tourist towns dotting the highway. With an open campus and five buildings spread around a courtyard, the main two-story building rose above the rest like a glorified and modern-day concrete box. Behind that was the gym and sports fields: a baseball diamond, a football field, tennis courts, and a running track. The gems of Benders High.

Velveeta told me they'd built the school three years earlier, and as I saw it, it had all the personality of a dead guy.

Clean lines, organized, institutional, and boring, Benders High, just like all the other new schools I'd seen, portrayed everything they expected its students to be: all the same and nothing to remember. If you took the signs down proclaiming it a school, it could be any government building built in the last ten years. I preferred to think of it as a low-risk detention center for nonviolent felons. Open and airy, but still a prison.

Velveeta left me with directions to my homeroom, which was B112, and I found it without much hassle. Compared to the other schools I'd gone to, Benders High was small. Tiny, really. The enrollment at the high school I'd left topped three thousand, and if you ever wanted to get lost, it was easy. Even after a year there, I still couldn't find some places.

I walked into the room, and twenty-three other sophomores talked and grouped and gathered in the usual huddles around the place. I took a second to look for the punker/skater/stoner/loser group and found a lone guy sitting at a desk in the back row of chairs.

Call me a conformist to nonconformity, but I sat next to him, setting my pack down and once again missing my friends back home. His hair was long, dark brown, straight, and feathered down his shoulders heavy-metal style. He wore an old-school Black Sabbath T-shirt. He looked at me, ran his eyes over my outfit, paused at my Converse All-Stars, then smirked. Green eyes. He looked like he should be in junior high. He tapped a pencil on the desk. "I'm infected; stay away."

33

"What?"

He gave me a droll look. "The Benders curse. It's contagious. You'll get it if you sit next to me."

I stared at him.

"My parents didn't stand in the genetic enhancement line before I was conceived."

I wondered if something about vineyards made people whacked in the head. "Are you insane?"

He shook his head, his voice lazy and lower than I would have figured. Sarcasm dripped around the edges. "No." He gestured to the students around the room. "Genetically altered peons. If you find one standing and staring blankly, wind them up and they'll start again."

I smiled. "Oh. I get it."

"Do you have a winder?"

"Not the last time I checked. What's your name?"

"Theo, but you can call me student number 31100."

"Poe."

He sat back, spreading his legs under the desk. "I've heard about you."

Oh God, it's already starting. "Small-town kind of thing?"

He smiled. "Privacy isn't in the Benders Hollow dictionary. You're the counselor's daughter. Let's see . . . Oh yeah, you're troubled. You know, disenfranchised from the franchise. That's what the engineers say anyway."

"The engineers?"

"Adults. The ones who program us. The winders of our winder things."

I knew from that second on, we'd get along just fine. "So what do they say about you?"

"Nothing anybody can hear. I'm invisible."

"Why is that?"

He blew his bangs out of his eyes. "My dad."

"Who is your dad?"

"The mayor. I'm exalted in my invisibleness."

I smiled. "Should I bow?"

"Only if you drop something."

"I take it you're not in the popular crowd?"

He laughed. "I'm in the no crowd. In the in because I'm a townie, but not in the in. Remember the curse?"

"What's the curse?"

"I was born with a polo shirt on and a golf club in my hand, but the doctor accidentally pushed the wrong button and I wound up with cognitive thought abilities. They don't like that around here, but since my dad is the mayor, they leave me alone. Invisible. If you stick around me too much, you become invisible, too. It's not that bad, but people tend to bump into you."

I smiled, the thought of being invisible not a bad one. "Got any glue?"

"Not that close. We wouldn't want anybody to think I actually have a life."

"Poor you."

"Not really. I'm a master at making lemons out of lemonade."

"That's backwards."

He looked at me, then glanced at the door. The teacher walked in. "No, it's not. I can turn anything sweet into sour. It comes with the territory."

Chapter Six

Being the new kid wore thin by third hour. I'd been the newbie before, and the looks, glances, snickers, whispered comments, and formal introductions to the class by teachers got old five seconds after it all started. Even though there were more than the usual share of clones at Benders High, I was disappointed to know that this school was pretty much the same as every other school I'd been to. I shouldn't have been surprised. School was like McDonald's. A Big Mac in Tulsa tasted exactly the same as one in Seattle, and there was a reason for it.

But third-hour current affairs was an exception to institutionalized indoctrination. No seating chart. Free seating. I knew the teacher must be taking a big chance with that one. People have a tendency to wander aimlessly when they have to decide something for themselves, and I figured half the class would be spent deciding. Theo was in that class, too, and when he came in, he plopped down next to me in the back row. He popped a piece of gum in his mouth. He could even chew gum sarcastically. "Want one?"

I nodded, taking a piece. "Thanks."

He slouched in his chair, bored with the world. "All the sheepherders making you feel comfy?"

"It can't be that bad around here."

"It's not. At least for me. I try to be as negative and depressed as possible about everything. It's hard sometimes, but hey, it's a job."

"Your job?"

"Yes, ma'am. My mother hasn't stopped smiling for seventeen years. She woke up one morning and her face stuck. Have you ever lived with somebody who's so happy it makes you want to eat your puke? Even my dad can't take that much sunshine, and he's the biggest glad-hander I know."

I laughed.

He nodded. "I'm serious. If I told her I wanted to slit my wrists up to my elbows, drink battery acid, and drive a car into a brick wall, she'd tell me to buckle up, have a good day, and grab a gallon of milk when I'm done. Reality and her don't go well together. I have to balance things out."

"Sounds weird." I glanced at the door, and Velveeta walked in.

"No," he said, pointing. "That's weird."

"He lives next door to us."

"I know."

I forgot how small this town was. "He's nice." I watched as Velveeta stopped at the entrance, scanning the room. His eyes didn't stop on me, though. They stopped on a guy in the front row near the windows. Their eyes met. Velveeta made a beeline to the farthest seat from him and sat down, and the guy shook his head and smirked.

"He's a lot of things."

I looked at Theo, and there wasn't any sarcasm there. "How's that?"

"You don't even want to know."

"Yeah, I do." At that point, the teacher walked in. A tall, pudgy man with a fifties-style businessman's haircut and dark eyes under thick eyebrows. He wore a white button-up shirt and navy blue tie.

"Ask your dad, then. That kid is in his office more than anybody in this school."

"His parents died in a car crash."

Theo looked at me. "Yeah."

The teacher stared at us, and I checked out my schedule. Mr. Halvorson. He cleared his throat. "Theo, since you seem to be talkative on this afternoon of the first day of school, perhaps you could introduce Ms. Holly to the class?"

Without pause, Theo stood, taking me by the arm and dragging me up. "This is Poe Holly. She's from Southern California, has a mommy and a daddy, likes skipping rope, eating crayons, drinking melted ice cream, and taking romantic strolls through the vineyards on warm summer evenings. She's joined the ranks of Benders High because she has a deep-seated need to be reduced to a mass of organic gelatin, compliments of the glorious administration and teaching staff of this wonderific and really special school. Furthermore..."

"That will be quite enough." Mr. Halvorson glowered. He looked at me. "Ms. Holly, welcome. Please take your seat." He picked up a piece of paper and handed it to the closest student. "Please fill in your name at the corresponding desk on the chart, then pass it along."

Fifty-five minutes of class rules, current affairs curriculum, and grade requirements later, we were dismissed. As I walked up the aisle, Mr. Halvorson called me aside. He waited a moment for the last of the students to exit the room, then leaned against his desk and smiled. "It is nice to have you here, Poe."

"Thank you."

He looked out the windows to the courtyard, then brought his eyes back to me. "I know being the new student is never easy, and I'm sure you're nervous with the first day, but I wanted to take you aside for a moment."

"Is there a problem?"

He smiled again. "Of course not. I take all new students aside to welcome them. You see, I believe in proactive approaches to teaching." He smiled, trying to hide his pride. "Some might call it aggressive, but this school is exceptional for a reason, and I'm dedicated to it." He studied me, his face warm and welcoming. "Are you getting along well in Benders Hollow? Fitting in?"

I nodded. "Sure. It's nice."

"Good. I wanted to talk to you about a program we have here. I happen to head it up." He glanced at the clock, collecting his thoughts before continuing. "I think many times it's easy for a student to fall into different categories and 'cliques' as you call them, and being the new student, oftentimes what happens is that you find yourself gravitating toward the easiest and most welcoming group. A group that you feel comfortable in, but perhaps a group that actually distances you from what Benders High School is all about." He glanced at my outfit, then went on when I didn't reply. "Anyway, I just wanted to let you know that as the head of the Benders High Committee of Equality and Fairness, we strive to provide a safe and productive environment for our students." He smiled. "I officially welcome you." He stopped, folding his arms across his chest when I didn't fall to my knees and worship him. He sounded like he was reading straight out of a handbook.

"Thanks, but I'm doing fine."

He nodded. "I'm sure you are, and you are obviously an intelligent young woman, but I think sometimes things are easier for those students who grasp the concept of team-work. That's what the committee is all about. We want this to be your home, and at home, comfort and positive atmos-pheres are important." He glanced out the door, where Theo was waiting for me. "We work hard at Benders High to of-fer students the opportunity to be part of the whole. To cast away the defensive mechanisms that create the subgroups that isolate students. Inside, we're all really the same, you know?"

I almost laughed. Homogenized diversity celebration. Communism with a spin. "Yes, I know what you mean. And thank you. I'll stay away from Theo. I can already tell he's not a team player."

He shook his head, frowning. "I wasn't alluding to any one person, Ms. Holly. My intent is only that you feel wel-come here, and I want nothing more than for things to go well for you and this school. And from experience, I know that sometimes having the courage to join in and be a part of something great is scary."

God, Theo wasn't exaggerating. I'd seen it before, but this guy dripped crap between the lines. "Thanks."

"Very well, then. And remember, come see me if you've anything on your mind. Perhaps I can help."

I walked out and shook my head. Theo walked beside me. "What?"

"Wow."

"Halvorson?"

"Yeah. He doesn't want me hanging around you."

"Oh, that. The anti-clique thing. Benders High prides itself on that. Halvorson has his own float during the Grape Days Parade."

"No way."

"Way." He laughed. "His idea of getting rid of cliques is to get everybody to join the best clique. He gave you the teamwork talk, didn't he?"

"Yep."

"Everything is fair and equitable if everybody is on the same team."

"And now you'll tell me what the best team is?"

"The good-people-that-wear-the-same-clothes-and-have-combed-hair clique. Sports, drama, the illustrious and award-winning choir, orchestra, chess, debate, anything with light and neutral colors that makes Benders High run like clockwork." He smiled. "You'd better find something quick or you'll be on the outside looking in. Oh, wait." He looked me up and down. "You're already on the outside. Sorry."

I didn't tell him about my deal with Dad. I'd be meeting with the choir teacher after school, and somehow Theo made me feel guilty about it. I glanced at the clock on the hall wall. "I've got to go. See you?"

He walked away, waving over his shoulder. "Sure thing."

The end of sixth period, math, finally came around, and I headed to the music building. The choir room was C102, and Mrs. Baird stood at a white chalkboard, wiping it down with a paper towel. Short highlighted hair cut into a prim bob, a dark blue knit sweater with a white turtleneck underneath, and beige slacks with low-heeled black shoes greeted me. A garish necklace around her slightly wattled neck was the only sign of creative flourish. A badge of rebellion. I stepped in the room. "Hi."

She turned around, looking me up and down. "Hello." She smiled. "You must be Poe. Your father told me you might be interested in choir."

I rolled my eyes. "Word travels quick around here."

She stepped up to me and shook my hand. "How was your first day?"

I shrugged. "Fine. Thanks."

She looked me up and down again, an insult under her friendly smile. I half expected her to stick her fingers in my mouth and check my gums. "So you're interested in singing?"

"I said I'd check it out."

She smiled warmly. "Well, do you sing in the shower? Everybody sings in the shower, right?"

"Yeah, I guess."

"We have a slot for you if you'd like. Depending on your range, that is. The main chorus is quite good. Not on the level of the Elite Choir, but they do quite well at competition."

My interest suddenly faded. "I don't sing well with others."

She raised her eyebrows, smiling. "Well, the choir is a group movement, as you know. Unless of course you're a soloist, but those spots are full."

42

I shrugged. "I am a soloist."

She furrowed her brow. "You know, Poe, it takes years of training to make soloist. The four soloists we have now have been singing since they were in kindergarten. In fact, we are one of the only schools in the nation to have soloist rankings. You're sure you wouldn't like to try the main chorus?"

"I'm sure." I looked to the door. "I've got to go. Bye."

She nodded. "Okay, then. Would you do me a favor, though?"

"What?"

"When I talked to your father and he told me you were in a little band of some sort, he asked that I listen to you sing before any decisions were made. Will you sing for me?"

I should have walked out, but I'd made a deal. Okay, I'm lying. I wanted to sing. I wanted to stuff it down her wattled throat. "Are you sure? I don't want to take up any of your time. I'm not trained professionally."

She led me further into the room, ignoring the jab as she sat at the piano. "Don't be so hard on yourself. The acoustics in here were specially designed, and they make anybody sound good. Why don't you step on the stage and take center." I stepped up, half tempted to sing in my best impression of Donald Duck. Then we'd see how these walls made me sound. She folded her hands in her lap at the piano. "What would you like to sing?"

I thought about it. " 'Bridge over Troubled Water,' by Simon and Garfunkel."

"A difficult piece."

I shrugged.

"All right, then. Take my lead."

"I don't need accompaniment."

She stared, smiled, then nodded. "Very well. Begin when it suits you."

Earlier and to a few oddball stares, I'd warmed up in the girls' bathroom. I was ready. I began, and just like always, twenty seconds into it I found myself lost to the real world. The only thing I knew was the feeling my voice gave me. Like if there was something perfect in this dirty world, I could find it through singing. Like I could blow down a building or stroke a butterfly wing with this song.

When I finally shut my trap and stopped singing, Mrs. Baird sat staring at me. The silence of the room finally gave way to her. "I'm afraid I owe you an apology."

I picked up my bag. "Not interested."

She stood. "I'm sorry. I didn't think . . ."

"I told you I'm not interested."

Flustered, she lurched forward, light in her eyes. "I want you in this choir as the lead soloist. In the Elite Choir. Your pitch was perfect, your range is incredible, and I didn't hear an off-key note. Not one. How many octaves can you range?"

"I don't have professional training, remember? It takes years."

A hint of anger lit her eyes. "I was just saying that the competition for those spots was intense."

"No, you weren't. You were saying I didn't have a chance in hell and the spots were already taken. You made that decision the second I walked in the door and you looked me up and down."

Her jaw tightened. "Well, they are taken. Or were. But

44

I'll not mince words. You're better than they are, and though you may not think so, I run my choir based solely on talent. Not politics."

I smiled. "Five minutes ago I was a waste of your time."

She ignored it. "We'll call today a late tryout. A walk-on."

"No."

"Why not?"

"I told you why not."

"I'm not going to beg, Poe. You'll be wasting an incredible talent if you walk out that door. I can get you recognized. You can have a future."

"I don't want your kind of recognition or your kind of future, thank you."

"Poe . . ."

I shook my head. She wasn't that bad, but this wasn't for me. I didn't deal with school politics and bullshit, and that's why every school I ever went to had me in at the first ring of the bell and out at the last. "I had an agreement with my dad, Mrs. Baird, and I did it. I'm not singing in your choir."

She nodded, upset. "Okay, then."

・　・　・

As I walked from the school grounds, I didn't feel good about anything. The way she'd looked at me when I first walked in was nothing new. I got that from teachers constantly, but it still made me feel like a lump of crap. Some teachers loved and lived on having contempt for students.

I imagined myself in one of their silly robes, front and center at a competition and singing my heart out, and I didn't laugh at it. I knew I'd like it. I would. I'd like the feeling, because that's what singing was all about. But I wasn't about to be a part of something that every grain of my being was against, and the name of the varsity choir, the Elite, said it all. If you didn't look the part and play the part and have all the proper pedigrees, you were nothing.

I wasn't nothing, though. I could sing, and now the tables were turned. I shut her out and made her feel like crap just like she went around doing to other people. She could take her professionally trained hand puppets and stick them up her big butt for all I cared.

I turned the first corner from the school and saw Velveeta walking a block up, his lanky gait recognizable even from this distance. I quickened my pace, hoping to catch him before we got home, but then he took a left through a large vacant lot and disappeared.

As I approached the overgrown lot, I saw the path he'd gone down and followed, thinking it was a shortcut. As I entered the narrow path, I saw the flash of his T-shirt before he disappeared around the brush thirty yards ahead.

Then I heard muffled voices. I slowed, not sneaking, but interested in what was going on, and rounded the corner. Maybe he was scoring some dope or something. The path straightened from there on, with the backyard fences of houses on one side and the brush on the other. Velveeta stood in front of two guys, both of them big, and the smiles on their faces weren't friendly.

I stopped, watching as they talked. I couldn't hear what was being said, but Velveeta held a piece of paper in his hand and kept gesturing to it. Then one of them laughed, ripping the paper away and crumpling it up. He threw it on the ground, then pointed, directing Velveeta to pick it up.

Velveeta shuffled, and this time I heard the guy order him to pick it up.

As Velveeta bent, the bigger of the two pounced on his back and smashed him to the ground, pinning his neck with his palm. With Velveeta's cheek pressed against the dirt and the crumpled paper in front of him, the other guy squatted down and laughed. "Eat it, cheese head."

My stomach did somersaults, and I knew I should do something. I didn't, though. I couldn't. I don't know why. My feet froze to the path. I could only watch as one of the guys picked up the paper and forced it into Velveeta's mouth. "Chew it, bitch. Take it down, boy. That's right. Eat it."

With the paper stuffed halfway into his mouth, Velveeta refused to chew. The kid pinning him pressed harder on his neck. Velveeta grunted, and his body, sprawled on the ground, tightened spastically, resisting the pressure. Tears welled in my eyes, but I couldn't do it. I couldn't tell them to stop, but like a car wreck, I couldn't stop watching, either. Velveeta chewed. They laughed. "Choke it down, retard. Oh yeah. Did your dead bitch of a mother feed you like this, you desert pig?" the one on top said, then ordered him to swallow it.

Velveeta didn't, and this time, the kid squatting in front of his face reared back and punched his forehead, the dull thud reaching my ears. I stepped out and yelled, screaming my head off with every cussword known to man coming out. They sprang up, staring at the screaming crazy loon for a few seconds before flipping me off and strutting down the path laughing. Velveeta lay still.

I walked to him, not wanting to be here, but not able to

leave. I didn't want to see this. Nobody should see this. I knelt. His breath came in sharp rasps, eyes wide and staring at nothing as drool from the corner of his lip puddled in the dirt. His cheek bulged with the paper, and like a slow-motion movie scene, he parted his lips and the mushed-up contents plopped out, filaments of slobber running streams from it to his mouth. He didn't move. I looked away. "Are you okay?"

He didn't answer, and as I knelt further and put my hand on his shoulder, he flinched. I took my hand away. His breathing calmed, but his eyes remained fixed on nothing. "Go away."

I stood, picked up his backpack, set it beside him, and looked at anything but him. "I'm sorry."

He didn't reply, just lay there, and I left.

Chapter Seven

Dad was home by four-thirty, and I avoided him. I couldn't get Velveeta out of my head, and it bothered me. I'd seen kids picked on and beaten up and harassed. Every kid has, and I'd even been targeted once or twice. But I wasn't one of those dweebs running around talking about how traumatized I was and how the healing needed to begin.

My general outlook on life was that shit happened, and if you didn't have the guts to take care of business, you deserved it. That's why I was so bothered by why I was so bothered. Any reality-based person who looked at Velveeta knew he took crap from other kids. And adults. Some people were born to be picked on, and he was one of them. That's the way the world worked, and no matter what anybody tried to do about stopping it, they couldn't. The strong preyed on the weak, the smart preyed on the dumb, and the smarter stayed away from it all. Human beings were cruel creatures.

What bothered me so much about Velveeta was the way he'd taken it. The way he lay still with his eyes wide reminded me of how an antelope looked when a pack of lions attacked it. Sure, he'd been defiant by refusing to swallow the paper, just like an antelope will run until the jaws close around its neck. But just like the antelope finally standing still as the jaws clamp and the claws rake its flesh away, there'd been an air of resignation around it all. Those staring eyes just waiting for it to be over. Like he knew this was supposed to happen and it was natural for it to happen to him.

It made me sick. I'd seen guys kicked in the head and put into comas during fights at raves and parties, and it hadn't bothered me as much. This time, those two lions hadn't pulled down their prey for any other reason than entertainment, and I'd stood there and watched it.

I walked outside just before dinner and sat on the porch.

"Thanks."

I turned. Velveeta stood at the fence. He had a lump on his forehead from the hit. I didn't know what to say, so I said what was on my mind. "Why'd they do it?"

He shrugged it off. "They were just funning around. You know, guy stuff."

"No, I don't know."

He grinned, but it wasn't all there. "Aw, guys do that kind of stuff to each other. Heck, I've even done it."

I looked at him. "I think I know when somebody is full of shit."

He turned a shade of red, looking along the fence. "Okay, fine. Maybe I haven't, but it was just a joke. That's all. They razz me sometimes."

"That wasn't razzing."

His face fell for a moment. "Well, you shouldn't have

been following me in the first place, so it's not your business anyway."

I shook my head, my thoughts on that antelope. "Why didn't you fight?"

He shrugged, looking away.

"They'll keep doing it, you know."

He smiled. "More'n one way to fight, I suppose."

"What's that supposed to mean?"

His grin widened. "Wouldn't you like to know."

The last thing I was interested in was more macho bullshit. "Not really."

His grin disappeared.

"What was the paper all about?"

He shuffled. "It was a note."

"From who?"

He sighed. "You just won't quit, will you?"

"It was all in fun, right? So tell me."

He shrugged, looking off down the street. "There's this hot girl at school. Her name is Anna Conrad. She wrote it."

"What did it say?"

"It don't matter."

"Tell me."

He guffawed. "Aw, man. It said she liked me and stuff, but that she couldn't come and tell me so. She told me to meet her in the lot after school so we could talk. It was a joke is all. Ha ha. I'm the sucker. Big deal."

Anna Conrad became an instant member on my hate list. I'd known girls like her. "I thought you had a girl."

He smiled sheepishly. "Anna Conrad is really pretty."

"Pig." It came out automatic, and I regretted it the second I said it, remembering that one of the guys called him a desert pig. I also knew he didn't have a girl back home unless she had four legs and a cotton tail.

His eyes darkened, then the look disappeared just as quickly. "I always say it's worth a shot. Man's gotta keep his options open."

Just then, my dad came out the door. He looked at Velveeta. "Hello, Andrew. How was the first day of school?"

The goofy grin came back, like a dumb blonde who just might not be dumb. "Just fine, Mr. Holly. Back to the books is what they say, right?"

Dad smiled. "That they do." He looked at me. "Dinner's on, Poe." He nodded good night to Velveeta and went inside.

I stood, looking at Velveeta. Something about this guy made me want to be around him. Maybe it was because he said things other people didn't say. I studied him for a minute more. No, it wasn't what he said. It was what he didn't say, only giving tendrils and sound bites to who he really was. *More'n one way to fight, I suppose*, he'd said. Velveeta wasn't a dumb redneck, I realized, he was smart, and he was a mystery. "Are we walking tomorrow?"

"Sure."

"See you then."

He waved like a dork, grinning from ear to ear. "Bye."

• • •

We'd eaten in the formal dining room every night since I'd arrived, and as I walked to the kitchen to help dish, I looked toward the den. "Do we have to eat in the dining room every night?"

Dad stopped. "No. Why?"

"It's just so big. Like there should be more people or something. I'm used to eating in front of the TV."

He nodded. "Then the den it is."

"Where did you eat before I came?"

"Usually in my study."

I heaped my plate with rice and steamed vegetables, then dished some onto Dad's plate. He took two chicken breasts from the oven and forked them next to our sides. I sniffed. "Smells good. We didn't eat real cooked food that much."

"Thanks. The white sauce is my specialty." He opened a cupboard. "You get napkins and I'll get glasses. Water?"

"Sure. Unless you've got beer."

He smiled. "Yes, I do, but not for you."

"Worth a try."

. . .

I clicked on the TV and turned it to FOX News, and Dad came in a minute later. "You like the news?"

I nodded, taking my glass and giving him a napkin. "Yeah. I got into the habit of watching it for a class I had last year. We had to report on what was going on in the world. I like FOX. Bill O'Reilly is funny."

He smiled, picking up his fork. "I'm afraid I don't watch the news."

"You don't know who Bill is?"

"Afraid not."

"You must be a hermit. He's like the black sheep of the news. They all hate him."

"And that's why you like him, I take it."

"Yep. No fear, and he says what he believes, not what he believes other people think he should believe."

He took a drink, blinking. "I think I understand that. Are you a liberal or a conservative?"

"Neither. They're all crooked, but I like knowing what they're crooked about."

He laughed, cutting his chicken. "I see the apple didn't fall far from the tree."

I looked crossways at him, baffled. "Mom?" My mother didn't have a political bone in her body.

He shook his head. "Me. That's why I don't watch the news. I can't stand politicians."

That was the difference between him and me, I thought. When he didn't like something, he hid from it. I couldn't. Some intangible rage in me wouldn't allow it. "I met the mayor's son today. Theo."

He nodded. "That kid is a political statement if I've ever seen one."

I stared at him. "I thought you were supposed to be nice and all that. You know, the counselor thing. No real opinion."

He smiled. "Well, first of all, it wasn't a bad thing, and second of all, I do have an opinion on people. He's a smart kid. Smarter than most adults."

"What's your opinion on Velveeta?"

He paused, staring at the television for a moment. "Velveeta has gone through a tough time."

"He told me his parents died in a car crash."

He took a bite, chewed, and swallowed.

"They didn't, did they?"

He hesitated. "What did you hear?"

"Nothing, really."

He stopped, studying me for a moment. "They did die, Poe, but not in a crash."

"How?"

"They were manufacturing methamphetamine in their

kitchen and it exploded. They burned to death. Velveeta barely made it out of the house."

"Oh."

He turned to me, the leather of his seat squeaking. "Poe, Velveeta has some issues to deal with, and I'm asking you to be careful around him. That's just between you and me, okay? This is the dad talking."

"What happened?"

He sat back. "Velveeta has all but taken care of himself since he was a young boy, Poe, and with that comes emotional confusion. When a child is abused and neglected to the degree that he was, wires get crossed. Especially concerning relationships."

I frowned. "So he's wasted youth and I should stay away from him? Is that what you're saying?"

"No, I'm not saying that. I'm saying I'm concerned about you. Velveeta is very passive-aggressive and can be manipulative."

I laughed. "You mean he's learned how to survive in a world that shit on him? Who isn't manipulative? Who doesn't protect themselves in any way they can figure out?"

He smiled, then conceded with a nod. "Yes, basically. He has a good heart, Poe, but he's never been given the opportunity to learn how to use it."

"So what you're saying is that he should be given the opportunity to learn how to have a friend, but I shouldn't be the one to give him a chance." I shrugged. "That's a load of crap."

"No, it's not a load of crap. It's a concerned parent with priorities, you being on the top of the list."

I looked at him, and my anger faded. "Fair enough. But I'm not going to crap on him like everybody else in this town does."

"What?"

I told him what happened that afternoon. "Those guys are asses."

"I know that Velveeta is teased, but . . ." He paused. "Who were they?"

"I don't know, but you can't do anything about it. I told you as my dad, not the counselor."

"Poe . . ."

"No way. If he wants to bring it up during one of your powwows with him, fine, but you can't do that to me."

He nodded. "I understand. What I hear in this house is between you and me, and vice versa. Deal?"

"Deal."

I ate my dinner, and we watched the news for a few minutes. Dad finished, wiped his mouth, and patted his stomach. "Full."

I took another bite of chicken. "Almost there."

"You eat a lot."

"I'm not fat."

"No, I'm just saying that for somebody so small, you can pack it down."

I laughed. "I'm growing."

"Did you see Mrs. Baird today?"

I'd hoped he wouldn't bring it up. "Yes."

"How did things go?"

I shrugged.

"Not well?"

"Depends on who you ask."

"What happened?"

"Let's just say I'm not in the choir."

He furrowed his brow. "I may not be a good judge on singing, but I can't believe you wouldn't fit right in."

I rolled my eyes. "Oh, I don't fit in, all right."

"Did you sing for her?"

I nodded.

"What did she say?"

"She said I had the most awesome voice she'd ever heard."

He frowned. "Then what am I not understanding? You chose not to?"

"Yep."

"Why?"

I shook my head. "I don't want to talk about it."

"I thought we . . ."

"We did, and I did it. I went and checked it out. End of story."

He cleared his throat, thinking, then nodded to himself. "Well, thank you for checking it out, then."

This was so new to me. My mom would have bugged the crap out of me until I coughed it up, then would have spent a lifetime telling me why I wasn't doing things right. "She made me mad."

"How so?"

"The usual. After I walked in the room and she decided I didn't look like I'd fit in her little group, she went into this whole bullshit thing about professional training and why all of the soloists were so good and everything. Then I sang, and she was like, 'I need you, Poe. You could walk right on. I could give you a future.' "

He crossed his leg over his knee, taking the counselor position. "And you don't like that."

I rolled my eyes. I didn't need counseling, I needed a steamroller. "I don't need some lady shining me on with a load of bull before she even hears me sing. She can take her trained monkeys and pound sand."

He laughed. "Whoa. A bit of hostility, Poe?"

"No. It's just standard procedure for teachers."

"How?"

"They think they can treat you like an idiot because you won't get it. Like it's some sophisticated game that we're too dumb to understand. She decided I didn't fit into her clique, then had to backtrack when she realized I could do something for her."

"I don't know that to be true."

I thought about Mr. Halvorson. "Come on, Dad. Get real. Everybody thinks that cliques and all that stuff are because of the students, but that's not it. It's the school. I knew exactly what she was doing when I walked in that room, and it's the same thing with cliques. She put me in my place before I opened my mouth. So did Mr. Halvorson today after class."

"Mr. Halvorson?"

I shook my head. "It doesn't matter. What I'm trying to say is that schools are the most hypocritical things there are."

"I don't necessarily agree. Our society . . ."

"Baloney, and I'll prove it. Halvorson tells me that Benders High is anti-clique, but the only reason he's talking to me is because he already put me in one that he doesn't like. Then I walk into Mrs. Baird's class, she looks me up and down, decides I couldn't possibly fit in her little elite clique, then uses soft words to tell me I don't belong before

I even sing. That's not judging? That's not condoning a clique mentality? At least kids are honest about it."

"Honest?"

"Yeah. Mrs. Baird has to twist her words to let me know she doesn't want me in her little clique. If she'd been honest about how she thinks, she would have said that I couldn't possibly belong to such a great group of singers because I don't look the part, and of course I couldn't have professional training because I'm a scumbag."

"But she didn't say that."

I rolled my eyes. "That's exactly what she said. She just tried to say it in a way that a stupid teenager wouldn't understand."

"What reason would she have to do that?"

I got up, taking my plate. "Because she decided where I belonged before I opened my mouth, that's why. And that"—I smiled primly—"makes me right."

"Would you like me to talk to her?"

"What are you going to change? Human nature?" I was on a roll, and as I stood there, I decided to pursue it. "So, you don't agree that teachers are the ones who create cliques?"

"Society as a whole creates divisions."

"Yeah, and that's what makes us different from each other, which is what I like. I just don't like people who do it to hurt people."

He frowned. "What are you saying?"

"Teachers are supposed to lead us and show us we can be anything we're willing to work for *before* society puts us in our places based on our habits or looks. But they don't. They start it."

"How so?"

"Look at sports."

"What about them?"

"How did the skateboard team do last year at Benders High?"

He furrowed his brow. "There is no skateboard team."

I shrugged. "I saw at least fifteen guys carrying boards around just in one day of school."

"Poe..."

"The only thing I saw was a bunch of signs posted around campus saying NO SKATEBOARDING. Why?"

"Because it's a liability. If somebody gets hurt..."

"Exactly. Just like if a bunch of guys played baseball in the parking lot every day, they'd be a liability, too. NO BASEBALL signs would be posted," I said, then smiled. "But I guess the school pays out the butt to make baseball players feel special. They've got a team, a diamond, uniforms, all that."

"It's our national pastime, Poe. Come on."

I waggled my finger at him, smiling. "I'm not saying get rid of baseball, Dad. I'm saying don't use *tradition* as an excuse to ignore a sport with more participants. There's more skateboarders in high schools than baseball players, and so what does Benders High do? Heck, they don't just ignore them, they make it against the rules to do it, because there's no reason other than favoritism that a sport more popular than baseball should get zero support or money." I shrugged. "The very people who say that we're all equal are showing everybody that we're not. If that isn't creating negative stereotypes, I don't know what is." I paused. "It was the same with choir today, too."

"How so?"

60

I gestured to myself. "Look at me, okay? Any honest person would judge that I'm counterculture. Maybe rebellious. An independent thinker and a general pain in the rear, right? Well, guess what? I am, and honestly, part of the reason I look this way is to be judged exactly that way, and I accept it. But how does that equate to having no talent or goals or aspirations? That lady looked at me and figured right, Dad, but she tacked on the same stuff that your school tacks onto skateboarders, and it screams hypocrisy. And the school's solution to the problem is saying we shouldn't judge at all and that we're all the same, which is stupid. I want to be different, but somehow looking the way I do translates to not being able to sing. Who created that, counselor? Me or my teacher?"

He shook his head. "But you can't blame everything on other people, Poe. Your own attitude probably had something to do with her judgment of you, and that's fair."

I rolled my eyes. "When you tell somebody over and over again that they aren't worth anything, they generally don't like you for it. Maybe I'd treat her differently if she treated me differently."

"But people won't always do that, Poe. You can't expect . . ."

"I'm not talking about Joe Schmoe on the street! I can handle them. I'm talking about the people that supposedly exist in *children's* lives to show *children* what they're capable of! TEACHERS!" I smirked.

"It's a natural human trait to find categories for people, Poe. If you aren't traditional, you will be judged more harshly. Mrs. Baird did do the right thing after you performed. She told you that it didn't matter what you looked like and that you were welcome. She based her decision entirely on your talent."

"What if I didn't know I was good? What if I was insecure? I would have walked right out of that room without singing, Dad, just like I'm sure other students have. And you're telling me she did the right thing!"

Here I was fully enjoying the debate, and he was as calm as still water. He went on. "I see your point, but it's that way in the working world, too. An employer will judge immediately, and if you don't fall within the boundaries of what they find acceptable, you will lose. That's why we have standards. Some good and some bad."

I laughed. I'd heard the *school is just like a job* argument from my mom for years. "Last time I heard, it was an employer's *job* to judge who is best for their business, because it's *their* business. What you're saying is that it's a teacher's job to judge who is best for their school?"

He stopped, thinking, then sighed. "You got me on that one, but not all teachers judge like that. You've never had a good teacher?"

I grunted. "Of course I have. And I'm not saying that a good teacher even has to like me. Just don't put my head in a vise and grab a sledgehammer."

Finally, a bit of a spark in his eyes. "Good. I was afraid you were generalizing."

I laughed. "Mr. Trillmane, seventh-grade English. He totally fought for getting not crappy books for us to read on the school list. Totally cool. He let me write three reports in poetry format because he knew I loved writing songs." I smiled, remembering him. "He always said the only purpose the English language had was to communicate."

Dad nodded, smiling. "Think about giving Mrs. Baird a second chance? She did end up coming through, and she's a fantastic teacher." His eyes twinkled. "In my opinion, that is."

"Why would I?"

He smiled again. "Because first of all, it might not be worth hurting yourself to hurt her, and second of all, I'd like to sit in the audience and say, 'That's my daughter up there.' Then I'd like to stand up and clap like a big goofball. Like in the movies."

My breath caught, and I exhaled, all the fire gone from our debate. "How do you do that?"

"Do what?"

"Here I was all pissed off and enjoying our argument, and now it's gone. It's not fair. We're supposed to not talk to each other for three days now."

He shrugged. "Sorry."

I stood there for a moment, holding my plate, and he turned his eyes away uncomfortably. "I'll think about it."

He shifted, staring at the TV. "Night."

Chapter Eight

Two days later, I found out the names of the guys who made Velveeta eat the paper. Ron Jameson and Colby Morris. Colby Morris was the guy in third-period current affairs that Velveeta avoided the first day. Colby Morris, asshole of the year. He gave me a hard stare when I walked into class, finally realizing I'd been the girl in the lot. I flipped him off.

Theo walked with me after the hour was up, and I asked him about Colby. He smiled. "Our resident god. You might have to wear sunglasses around him. The halo gets bright. Especially after a win."

"A win?"

"Football, my little innocent. He's the star receiver. He caught for five billion yards last year and attained the 'most likely to live in the past when you're thirty years old award.' You know, one of those guys sitting on a barstool talking about the halcyon days of glory back in high school."

"Oh." I wasn't about to mention what happened to Velveeta.

Theo wore an Iron Maiden T-shirt today, and he looked cute. He slid me a glance. "Why? Got a crush on him?"

"Hardly. Just wondering."

He laughed. "Whatever."

"What if I do have a crush on him?"

He shook his head. "Then you have a nice way of show-ing it. I saw you give him the finger."

We walked.

"Something happen to make you give him the bird?"

"No."

"Awesome. I love people that randomly flip off strangers."

"Not to me. Someone else."

He sighed. "Velveeta."

"How'd you know?"

"There's nothing not to know. Colby Morris makes a sport of it."

"A sport of picking on him?"

He nodded. "Ever since he got here last year, some of the guys saw some fun in him. The kid is a magnet for that kind of shit."

"The whole school is in on it?"

He smiled. "Yeah, but Colby is the main one. And the vacant lot is the gossip of the day. The paper thing. Velveeta's the school entertainment."

I frowned. "I was starting to like you."

"What did I do?"

"You think it's funny."

"No, I think it's pitiful, but look at the guy, Poe. He aches for those guys to walk all over him, and Colby Morris is a natural at things like that. At least now. He used to be cool."

"And you just sit there and laugh."

"No, I don't. But you can't stop it. God, some weeks it happens every day."

"Yeah, but I don't have to like it."

He smirked. "Well, then, maybe you could borrow some halo polish from Colby, Mother Teresa."

"That's totally uncool, Theo. You don't have to sit there and gloat."

He smiled. "Take a breath. I don't like it either, but what am I supposed to do? Talk to Mr. Halvorson about it? Have a sit-in for anti-harassment? Jesus, Poe, this place was like a vacuum waiting for a guy like Velveeta to show up. It's unstoppable."

"And I suppose the school doesn't do anything?"

"Look around. This place is status quo central. It ain't a problem if the problem doesn't matter."

"Great."

"Listen, if my dad being the mayor has taught me anything, it's that the system works a certain way for a reason. It's not just evil by chance. It's the worldview."

"Worldview?"

"Yeah. We're not individuals, girl. We're a unit. The philosophy of collective fucked-upedness. See, if the unit as a whole is operating in a cool way, as the unit known as Benders High is, there are no problems. Velveeta is but a small glitch in the system of pumping out mindless world villagers to be productive members of society. Karl Marx had a point, you know? Give 'em a test or ten, tell 'em what they're good at, and bam, you've got your workforce. Velveeta is a minor distraction from the work of creating robots."

"You sound like an anarchist."

"Better than being a social communist."

"True. But we need school for, like, uh, being able to read?" A jolt of shame went through me. Was Poe Holly actually defending an institution? I decided that Theo was so far out there that he was the one that needed reeling in. He made me look like a pansy when it came to counterculture attitude.

"School is just like church. The core is good, but it's all the stupid parts that make it stupid."

"Brilliant, Theo." I rolled my eyes. "Stupid things generally make things stupid."

"Good, then we agree. Does that mean I can take you out for a burger after school?"

"Are you asking me on a date?"

He shook his head. "I don't believe in dating. I believe in casual encounters with other worker bees."

"I feel special."

He rolled his eyes. "I'm joking. Why don't we call it a pre-date? I'm still not sure you're good enough for me. I am the mayor's son, after all."

After school, Theo met me at the flagpole and we walked toward town, talking about music and politics and everything else that I liked. I felt like I'd known him all my life. Like we were conjoined twins or something. He loved music with a passion, all classic heavy metal. Judas Priest, Motley Crüe, Iron Maiden, Black Sabbath, old Metallica (before they sold out, he said), and Motorhead. He also told me he wanted to be a political satirist. A natural slide in, he said, because of watching his dad operate.

As we walked through the neighborhood, Velveeta turned the corner ahead of us, heading home. I watched him for a moment, and a pang of sickening pity accompanied the fire in my belly over my dad telling me not to hang out with him. "Mind if we invite him?"

Theo looked at the gangly stork walking. "I thought this was a pre-date."

"Come on. Give him a chance. He's actually really nice."

He shrugged. "Sure."

I called to him and he stopped, turning around. He grinned as we neared, scratching his ear. "Hi, Poe." Then he looked at Theo. "Hi."

Theo held out his hand. "Theo."

Velveeta didn't smile. "I know. Seen you about a million times at school."

"We've never really met."

I cut in. "We're getting burgers. Want to come?"

He looked down the street. "Burgers?"

"Yeah. Hungry?"

He thought about it for a minute. "Naw, you go. I got stuff to do."

I thought about the vacant lot. "Come on, it'll be fun. You can do your stuff later."

He shuffled. "You sure?"

I nodded. "Yeah. I'm starving. Come on."

He smiled. "Okay. I don't got money, though. Can I borrow some till tonight? My stash is at home."

Theo smiled. "Your stash?"

He nodded. "Yeah. My bank."

Theo sighed. "Oh. Got ya."

The burger place, off the main tourist strip and a local hangout, was full of kids. Velveeta shuffled, nervous. Arnie's, Home of the Big'un, was a hopping place. We ordered, got our food, and sat down. I popped a fry in my mouth before we started eating, looking at Theo. "You like it here?"

"No. But I wanted to impress you with how mainstream I was."

"Right."

"Actually, I'm a burger junky. I LOVE Arnie's burgers. Live on 'em if I could."

I smiled, flirting. I didn't even know I knew how to flirt. "So the real anarchist comes out."

He leaned back, stretching. "You know me. I'll stand up for any cause if it's easy, fun, and irritating to people. Principles get in the way of hedonism and personal pleasure."

Velveeta took the top bun from his burger, dug in his pocket, brought out a crumpled ball of tinfoil, opened it, took a chunk of warm, oily yellow cheese from it, plopped it on top of the cheese already there, and squished the bun back on. Theo and I stared. Then he opened his mouth wider than I thought humanly possible and took a bite. He chewed a few times, then looked at us, mayonnaise gathered at the corners of his mouth. "What's hedonism?"

Theo gaped at him. "What the fuck? Jesus, man, was that cheese?"

Cheeks stuffed with burger, Velveeta frowned. A piece of lettuce stuck to his teeth. "Yeah. Had some left from lunch." He set the burger down, taking the lid off again and picking up the remaining part of the chunk. Mayonnaise and lettuce coated it. "Want some? It's good."

I laughed into my fries, getting a kick out of Theo's expression. "He likes cheese."

Theo smiled. "There's a difference between liking and a fetish, dude."

Velveeta looked at the chunk of cheese in his hand, then put it on the paper beside the burger.

Theo frowned. "Dude, just put it back on. I was joking."

Velveeta put the lid back on his burger, keeping his eyes down. "Naw. I was just joking, too."

Theo looked at me apologetically, shrugged, then took a bite. "Hedonism means pure pleasure," he said.

Velveeta smiled again, back on track. "I heard of that. Like in the *Girls Gone Wild* videos. They got all kinds of hedonism going on."

I raised my eyebrows. *"Girls Gone Wild?"*

"Yep. Got the whole collection. You can order 'em from the TV. Nothin' but a big old party all the time with girls in their bathing suits. Lotsa lesbos, too. You seen them, Theo?"

He smiled, glancing at me, then looking away. "Part of one. The ads are on all the time."

A moment of awkward silence followed before Velveeta looked around the restaurant, craning his neck from side to side. "You ever seen hooters before?"

We stared at him.

He nodded to himself, still looking around. "This place is sorta like that. 'Cept there's no girl waitresses and they don't have uniforms like that. Those red shorts and tank top things."

I breathed, and Theo laughed. "Yeah, I've been to Hooters. Last summer in LA."

"You can order triple cheese on anything you want, and the hooter girls smile at you no matter what you look like.

Part of the job, I guess, on account of Mr. Hooter, probably. My dad told me it was good customer service."

The bell over the front door chimed, and three girls walked to the counter. One wore a cheerleader outfit, and the other two could have been glam twin rejects from that show *Malibu* that MTV vomited out weekly. Velveeta looked at them, the smile disappearing from his face as his eyes went to his lap. He shrank down a little bit. I frowned. "Who are they?"

Theo looked, then shook his head at me, mouthing "no." Velveeta kept his eyes on his lap. Theo drank the rest of his pop. "Let's skate, huh? I'm done."

I looked at his half-eaten burger, then at Velveeta's, then at the girls in line. Theo frowned. "Let's go."

Velveeta rose, and I did, too. Theo led the way, and as we passed behind the Cosmo twins, they looked at Velveeta and laughed. In another few seconds, we were outside. Velveeta walked four or five steps ahead of us. I walked beside Theo. "Who were they?"

"The one in the cheerleader outfit was Anna Conrad."

I frowned, out of the loop. Then I remembered. The note. She'd written it to Velveeta. "Oh."

Theo grunted. "Queen socialite of Benders High. I think she's slept with every guy in five counties."

"Including you?"

He shook his head. "Nope. She stays away from me."

"Why?"

"Because her dad ran against my dad one year. For mayor. My dad crushed him."

I watched Velveeta walk, his hands stuffed in his pockets and his shoulders hunched. "This town is a soap opera. God."

"You've got that right. And Anna is the singing angel in the center of it."

"What?"

"She's the lead soloist in the Elite Choir. Actually, she's awesome. I heard her sing at the wine festival after the parade last year. Last I heard, she qualified for some national contest in Philadelphia."

That set me back, and I had a flash of jealousy. Anna Conrad would have been second string to me if I'd taken the soloist position. "Great."

"Oh, it gets better. Her mother chairs the school board committee. Funding isn't a problem for the choir." He smiled. "It also helps that her mom's one of the three judges that pick soloists every year."

"So I guess Anna is a walk-on, then?"

"Maybe if she didn't have a voice, but she's got some pipes on her."

I thought about that, then thought about what Mrs. Baird told me. She knew Anna would be second soloist if I took the spot, and she obviously wasn't afraid to deal with her mother about it. I watched Velveeta walk. "Hey, Velveeta."

He looked back.

"Slow down, huh?"

He did, and we all walked together. Theo hopped on the curb, balancing as he went. "Sorry about that, man."

"Sorry about what?"

"About Anna Conrad being there."

He frowned, definite friction between the two. "You got something to say to me?"

"I mean about the note and everything. Bad timing."

Velveeta looked at his feet. "What note?"

I nudged Theo, and he got the picture. "Nothing, man. No sweat. Those burgers are so big I can only eat half anyway."

We came to our houses and Velveeta waved us off, heading up his walk and disappearing in his front door. The Volvo was gone, Dad off doing something after school, and Theo and I found ourselves alone on the front porch. We sat, and after a moment, Theo spoke. "So, you like it here?"

"It's okay."

He nodded. "I always wanted to live in Los Angeles."

I laughed. "Yeah. It's cool. I miss it."

"Lot of friends?"

"No, not really. Just a few good ones."

"Must be hard coming here. With your dad and all."

I shrugged. "I never knew him. He's different."

"He's cool," Theo said.

I turned to him. "You think?"

"Yeah. You can't really talk to my dad. You say something, and he talks at you the rest of the time. It's the born leader in him. At least that's what he says."

"He sounds funny."

"He is. He's great. But he's like a bull in a china shop."

"My dad is like a gnat in the room. It's like pulling nails to get anything real out of him."

"All the surface counselor crap?"

"Yeah. Sometimes I feel like I'm reading a textbook when he talks."

"What's your mom do?"

"Avoid me."

"Ha. Really."

"She's a surgeon. In South America saving people for a year."

"Nice."

"If you like doing the right thing for the wrong reasons, sure."

"What's that supposed to mean?"

"It means that my mom really doesn't care about people in South America. She cares about herself and what she looks like to her high-society snoot doctor friends."

He frowned. "Listen, Poe, my dad is a politician. Your mom is a *doctor*. She saves people."

I looked at him. "Don't start with that, okay? I don't care what she is."

"Whoa. Danger ahead. Didn't mean anything by it."

"I know. I just don't want to talk about it, okay?"

Theo nodded, and just then, the Volvo rounded the corner. He stood. "Listen, I've got to split, and I can't really be seen around town with the school counselor." He smiled. "I've got my own image to maintain."

I laughed. "Chicken."

"Cluck cluck. See ya later."

Chapter Nine

After Theo left, I told my dad I forgot something at school and double-timed it back, hoping I wasn't too late. Mrs. Baird sat at her desk flipping through papers, and a girl, one I hadn't seen around campus, filed more papers into a cabinet near the stage. I knocked on the doorjamb, and Mrs. Baird looked up. "Oh, hello, Poe."

I stepped in, swallowing a big hunk of pride. "Hi. Do you have a minute?"

She stood, coming around her desk. "Sure. What can I do for you?"

I glanced at the girl filing papers, then walked further in. "Well, I've been thinking about what you said the other day. About singing."

She nodded. "Yes?"

Anna Conrad flashed through my mind, and I smiled. "I'll take the soloist position."

Chapter Ten

Chapter six of David's new self-help book, untitled as of yet, was about following through with ongoing issues. It basically means it's unhealthy to let something slide, because it will just fester and get worse. The road to recovery and understanding is communication, my father wrote. I sat on the front porch thinking about it. Pretty good, actually.

I heard the front screen open and looked to the side. He walked out with two cups of coffee in his hands. Still as the painting I'd imagined when I first arrived, the neighborhood was dark and silent. Not even a wisp of breeze. He held a cup out to me. "I put creamer in it."

I took it, tucking my feet under me and inhaling the scent of the hot liquid. "Thanks."

"Mind if I sit with you?"

I sipped. "Go ahead."

He did, and, as usual, was silent. You'd think that as a counselor, he would yap his head off all the time, but he never did. We talked, sure, but it wasn't the constant jabbering like with my mom. He crossed his leg over his knee. "Nice night. Sometimes you can almost smell the grapes."

I wondered how many nights he'd spent here in silence. Did he have a girlfriend? Friends? Was he truly a hermit? I breathed. "I thought you were gay when I first got here."

He cleared his throat. "Hmm. Why?"

"The house, and the other pair of sandals by the door."

He nodded. "Ah. I can see how you would wonder."

"Are you?"

He took a moment. "No."

A cricket sounded in the distance, followed by another. We watched a neighbor's car slide by slowly, the headlights piercing the darkness. "Why don't you ever answer anything?"

"I did answer, Poe."

"Not really. Not like real."

"I'm not a homosexual."

My voice came soft, silken with the night. "What are you, though? Before I got here, I mean? What did you do?"

"You mean my schedule? I would mostly come home and write."

"Do you have friends?"

He nodded. "I do. And I occasionally have them over."

"Women?"

"Occasionally."

"Girlfriend?"

"Not at the moment. I dated a nice woman from Northburg recently, though. You remember Northburg? We purchased your iPod there."

"What was her name?"

"Clara."

"How'd you meet?"

"She's an elementary school teacher. We met at a seminar."

"Was she nice?"

"Yes, she was." He looked at me. "Poe, is everything all right?"

I looked out into the darkness, hearing the crickets, feeling the coolness of the night. "Why did you leave?"

Moments passed. He didn't move, just sat staring out at the same thing I stared at. "Your mother and I found ourselves following different paths, and . . ."

"Please don't say that," I said into the stillness.

"What would you like to know, Poe?"

"Why you left *me*."

"I didn't leave you. . . . I left . . ." He stopped then, and the most uncomfortable silence I've ever felt followed.

"Did you just not love me?"

"No. Yes. I loved you. I've always loved you."

"Then why?"

He cleared his throat. Another car passed. "Poe, sometimes in this world, things just happen. Two people think they're in love, they make plans and have dreams, and then they realize mistakes have been made."

"Like having me?"

He reached across the little table and put his hand on my knee. I brushed it off. Then wiped my eyes. He took a deep breath. "No. Not you. You were never a mistake."

"Then answer me. Why did you leave? Why did I meet you in person sixteen years after you left? Why, Dad?" I wiped another tear, trying to hide it. Trying to keep this man who was my father a stranger. An outsider to be kept at a distance.

He looked straight ahead. "I've hurt you."

I sniffed. "I grew up wanting a dad so bad, you know? And Mom would never talk about it. Ever. Just the same old thing. You were gone. It didn't matter. We couldn't change the past. She never told me anything."

"I'm sorry, Poe. I never realized . . ." Then he stopped. He set his coffee next to mine. "I left because I was young and foolish and frightened. We were both in school, your mother was headed toward being the surgeon that she is today, and I was heading toward writing the great American novel. And we got married. Our romance was full of passion and freedom and all the things that I wanted and that I'd ever been told were normal and perfect, and with that, you came. But I was scared."

"Of what?"

"Of you, Poe."

I bent my head, staring at my lap. "Why?"

"I was scared of being a father and all of the things that go along with it, and your mother despised me for it. It was weak, I was weak, and so I did what I thought best at that time. I left."

"Did she want you to?"

"Yes."

"She still thinks that way about you. I can tell when I bring it up. Contempt. She treats me that way, too."

"Your mother is a strong woman. A woman with her opinions and her way of living. I didn't fit in with that, though I loved her and still do love her."

"So you left."

"Yes. I thought it would be better that I wasn't in your life."

"That's stupid."

"Yes, it is. And I've spent the last sixteen years being too ashamed of what I did to make it right. I've lived in this shell of a house trying to hide from myself, and then you came along, took that sledgehammer out, and pounded me on the head."

I closed my eyes. "I wish you never left." It came out a whisper, with the tears dripping from the tip of my nose and onto my folded hands.

There was nothing to say to that, so we sat, and he took my hand in his, and I let him.

Chapter Eleven

Physical education class took place two times a week at Benders High, and Friday rolled around with me heading toward the gym. Benders High had official physical education uniforms consisting of monogrammed sweats, shorts, and cheapo T-shirts. I looked terrific in my little outfit, and just being there made me want to become a pro volleyball player even though I was five foot one. I could barely touch the bottom of the net.

Mrs. Policheck, otherwise known by the original and apt title Coach, was the girls' instructor, and the gym was split in half, one side for the girls, the other side for the guys. I looked for Theo across the cavernous sports place but only saw Velveeta, dressed as I was in a dandy outfit.

A hundred or so other red-colored dweebs wandered around hitting balls over nets before class officially started, and as the sounds of twice-weekly active young people echoed through the building, I sat on the bleachers and watched Velveeta.

While most of the girls stood on the courts talking, most of the guys grouped on either side of the nets playing unorganized pickup games, spiking and bumping and setting. Velveeta stood on one of the courts as the balls sailed, shuffling toward balls that came close, then backing up when other guys swooped in to take them. Then I noticed something.

Dotted throughout the courts of red sweats and T-shirts were guys out of uniform from the top up. They wore their football jerseys. Apparently the regular Benders High T-shirts weren't good enough for them. I looked again at the girls. A few of them also had what looked like jerseys on from the volleyball and softball teams. As I watched, the boys' coach came in and blew his whistle. Heads turned, including Velveeta's, as balls fell to the floor. All except one.

On the opposite side of the net where Velveeta stood watching the coach, a guy in a jersey held a ball. Colby Morris. He tossed it up, then jumped, spiking it like a bullet over the net. It hit Velveeta square on the back, and down he went, arms and legs tangled in a heap. It had to hurt, and the smack echoed from all the way across the room. Laughter ratcheted through the building as Velveeta writhed on the court, arching his back in pain.

The coach blew his whistle, shook his head, then glanced at Velveeta. "Lines!" he bellowed, and guys scurried together as the coach walked toward the center of the courts. Another guy, this one in a red shirt, held out a hand to Velveeta to help him, and just as Velveeta was halfway up, the guy jerked his hand away, sending Velveeta sprawling on the hardwood floor again.

More laughter, and the coach turned, shaking his head at the interruption. He pointed to the kid who did it, then jabbed his finger to the bleachers. The kid shrugged, then walked and sat. A few seconds later, Coach Policheck came in and told us to line up, too. I walked up to her, that sinking feeling in my gut that said I shouldn't do what I was about to do. "May I use the bathroom?"

She smiled. "You must be Poe Holly. I'm Coach Policheck."

"Nice to meet you."

"Yes. Go ahead."

I went into the locker room, opened my locker, ditched my Benders High T-shirt, and put my own T-shirt back on. A black Sex Pistols tee with a red anarchy sign slashed across it. When I walked into the gym, Coach Policheck frowned. "You need to wear your uniform, Poe."

"No, I don't."

"Excuse me?"

"You don't have to wear your PE uniform."

"Yes, you do."

I pointed to the other side of the gym, to the football players, then swept my finger to the girls in their shiny jerseys. "They aren't."

She looked, then turned back to me. "Those are uniforms."

I looked down, smiling proudly like a complete idiot. "This is my uniform."

She set her jaw. The line of girls stood silent. "Young lady, I will have you change back into your uniform right now. Benders High School has a uniform policy for physical education."

"I am in my uniform."

She pointed to the football guys. "Those are Benders

High School uniforms, and they are acceptable attire for this class. Now go change."

I smiled. "I want one, then."

She tapped her foot. "Go change."

"No."

"If you don't change right this instant, you'll be sent to Vice Principal Avery's office."

I smiled, glancing at Velveeta across the gym. At this point, the guys had noticed what I was doing, and you could hear a pin drop as our voices vibrated through the building like a surround sound system. "Then maybe you should send me to the office."

Giggles broke out, and Coach Policheck pointed to the door. "Out. Mr. Avery will be notified of your arrival."

I walked into the locker room, slipped out of my sweats, got dressed, and left. The administration building sat across the courtyard, and as I walked, I thought about what I'd done. Four days into school and I'd already screwed it up. Figured. Poe Holly did one thing well, and this was it. They could go stuff themselves.

I entered the office thinking about Velveeta squirming around on the floor and the coach ignoring him. He *was* the school entertainment, just like Theo said, and as I faced the office assistant sitting behind the counter, I didn't feel one ounce of regret for what I'd done. A sign on the counter read *Ms. Appleway.* My eyes went from it to her. In her sixties, she looked like everybody's grandmother. "I'm here for an appointment with Mr. Avery."

She smiled, looking down. "Yes. Coach Policheck called to let us know you'd be coming. Apparently a problem with our uniforms?"

I smiled. "Not as far as I'm concerned."

She smiled wider, leaning closer and winking. "Good for you, kiddo."

I blinked, not believing she'd said it. I looked to a row of doors with seats by them. "Over there?"

She nodded. "He'll be with you in a moment."

I took a seat in one of the padded chairs outside the door with the sign reading *Vice Principal Avery,* and a moment after Ms. Appleway buzzed his office, the door opened.

Mr. Avery didn't have the usual suit and tie on that I was used to administrators strutting around in. He wore a pair of casual slacks and a polo shirt with *Benders High* stenciled on the left breast, and he weighed a good four hundred pounds. Ruddy cheeks blended into his neck, and his belly and hips flowed over his waistline like sacks of gelatin under his shirt. The indent of his belly button looked like a doughnut hole under the stretch of the fabric, and as he stood there, his volume left an inch or so of space to either side of the doorway. He hitched up his pants, sighed, looked at me, and smiled. "Ms. Holly? Please, come in." I stood, and he held out his hand. "I was hoping to meet you under different circumstances."

I shook his hand, then followed him into the office. Two chairs sat in front of his desk, and my dad was in one of them. I rolled my eyes as Mr. Avery squeezed past a filing cabinet and sat. He cleared his throat. "Please, take a seat."

Dad crossed his ankle over his knee. "Hello, Poe."

I slumped in the seat next to him. "So I get the third degree from the start, huh?"

Mr. Avery shook his head. "No, ma'am. Actually, your

father and I were having a meeting when the call came. It was opportune that he stay."

"For who?"

He glanced at my dad, then went on. "What seems to be the problem with your PE uniform?"

I shook my head. "I think Coach Policheck might be confused about the uniform policy."

Mr. Avery didn't buy it. "You refused to wear your uniform?"

"I was wearing my uniform."

"Coach Policheck notified me that you refused."

"Oh, you mean the crappy red thing? I put it on at first, but then when I realized you could wear cooler stuff, I changed."

He frowned, the pudge of his cheeks almost burying his eyes. "Cooler stuff?"

"Yeah. You don't have to wear the uniform I was given."

"You do, though. It's school policy."

"No, it's not."

He took a deep breath, glancing at my dad again.

"Why do you keep looking at my dad?"

"Excuse me?"

"You keep looking at my dad like you don't know what to do."

Dad spoke up. "I think Mr. Avery is having trouble understanding what the problem is, Poe. I think I know, but why don't you explain?"

I shrugged. "When I saw that you don't have to wear the PE uniform, I changed. Is there a problem with that?"

Mr. Avery swallowed. "Who wasn't wearing their uniform?"

"About ten or fifteen people. They were wearing different shirts."

A moment passed as he finally connected the dots. "Are you speaking of the sports uniforms?"

"I'm speaking of not having to wear the PE shirts."

He nodded. "Sports participants are allowed to wear their jerseys during physical education class."

"So some people do and some people don't?"

He shook his head. "Not exactly. They are Benders High uniforms, so we allow it."

"So it depends on who you are, then," I said, slowly turning my head to my dad and smirking.

Mr. Avery shook his head, wary. "Students may wear Benders High sports uniforms to PE."

"Cool. I want a football one to wear in PE. Theirs are nicer."

He looked at my dad. "I'm at a loss here, David. She's not on the football team."

Dad turned to me. "Poe, Mr. Avery is saying that if you have another uniform with the Benders High insignia, you are allowed to wear it to class because it is a Benders High uniform."

"I know. And I want a football one."

Mr. Avery cut in. "You can't, Poe. You don't play football."

"What do football jerseys have to do with PE? We're doing volleyball."

Mr. Avery lowered his voice. "You are welcome to try out for football, and if you make the team, you're welcome to wear the jersey to PE."

I rolled my eyes. "Are we done playing games yet? You

know exactly what I'm saying. The extracurricular sports heroes get to wear fifty-dollar PE uniforms and the losers get the six-dollar ones."

Mr. Avery shifted in his seat, staring at the desk. "It's not that way, really. They're the same."

"Cool. If they're the same, I want a football jersey." I smiled.

Mr. Avery's tone hardened. "You have to wear your uniform, Poe."

"But I want a super-duper one, like all the cool kids."

"Poe . . . ," Dad cut in.

I backed off. "Okay, Mr. Avery. Then just answer my question and I'll wear the uniform."

He sighed, folding his hands together on his desk and hunching. "And what would that question be?"

"That some people get to choose and some people don't, depending on your status here."

He sat back, totally frustrated. "Yes, you can wear a sports jersey if you play a sport at Benders High."

"You didn't answer."

"Poe . . ."

I shrugged. "Some people get to choose and some people don't, depending on your status here."

He threw his pen on the desk. "Okay, fine. Some students get to choose. Happy?"

I stood, smiling. "Just wanted to get things straight. Are we done?"

Mr. Avery nodded. "Will you wear your uniform, Poe?"

"Sure." I looked at my dad, then scratched my head. "What were we talking about the other night, Dad? Oh yeah. How schools don't create cliques."

Dad groaned. "Poe . . ."

I shook my head. "Sorry, I've got to go get my loser uniform back on and play volleyball with the special students. Bye." I walked out, leaving them sitting there. Two could play at this game, and I was just winding things up.

Chapter Twelve

After school, I hitched my bag over my shoulder and headed for the choir room, still gleefully simmering over my conversation with Mr. Avery. Choir practice began Monday morning before school, and Mrs. Baird wanted to give me the music I'd have to learn before then. I walked in the class, and she was alone. "Hi."

She looked up from her desk. "Hello, Poe. Thanks for stopping by." She shuffled through a file on her desk, then picked it up and handed it to me. Her eyes were tense, the lines around them drawn and tight. "I included an event calendar and all the paperwork you'll need to attend the various competitions. The fees are paid for by the school, so you won't have to worry about that. And . . ." She stood, opened a cabinet, and took out a package. "Here is your choir gown. It should fit, but if it doesn't, let me know and I'll get you another one. They're quite expensive, so be careful with it."

I looked at the plastic-wrapped and folded gown, in the red and black Benders colors and with the school signature emblazoned on it, and stuffed it in my pack. "Thanks. Monday morning at seven-thirty?"

"Yes. Monday, Wednesday, and Friday. I attended to your class schedule, too, if you don't mind, switching your elective to choir fourth period."

"Cool."

She nodded, and I was out the door, walking home and wondering what would greet me when I got there.

Dad wasn't around when I arrived, but Theo was. I hesitated when I saw him sitting on the porch steps. He smiled as I neared, then lounged back on his elbows. "You're my hero."

I unslung my bag and let it drop, plopping it on the ground and sitting. "Give me the definition of a hero and maybe I'll agree."

"A hero, as defined by *Webster's Unabridged Dictionary*, is a person who relentlessly pursues idiotic administrators and goofballs, putting herself in harm's way to expose the evil that lives within the systems we create to control people."

I smirked. "Evildoers. The president might be proud, but I'm not sure Mr. Avery is on the same level as rogue third world countries that want to develop nuclear weapons."

He shrugged, lazy in the afternoon sun. "It's all place and time, Poe. One man's Middle East is another woman's vice principal."

"Yeah, but Benders High isn't sitting on one of the world's largest oil fields."

"Come on, give yourself some credit. Word is you stood up to the beast and lived. What happened in his office?"

"Gossip gets around quick, huh?"

"Yep, so spill it."

"Nothing. I agreed to wear my loser uniform."

He gasped dramatically. "Where's the rebellion? The fire in your belly? God, if you're going to be a revolutionary, you can't cave in. It's very un-revolutionary-like. You're not some Gumby to be bent and twisted, are you?"

"I'm not interested in a revolution. The rule is stupid, so I said something."

"Stupid is as stupid does."

"My dad and I had talked about that kind of stuff, and I wanted to prove a point." I paused, thinking. "You just called yourself stupid."

"Moi?"

"You wear the T-shirt," I said. "Stupid rules for stupid people, right?"

"Got me. I just don't have the willpower to fix the system," Theo said.

I looked at my feet. "It was sort of stupid, I guess. Immature."

"No. It wasn't. Was your dad there?"

"Yeah. They just happened to be having a meeting when I came in."

He laughed. "What a coincidence."

"Yeah. I did get Mr. Avery to squirm, though."

"Seeing a fat man squirm can be an ugly thing."

I smiled. "I suppose so. He seemed pretty nice, really."

"He is, and that's the problem. It would be easy if the purveyors of social inequity were all assholes, but they're not, and what makes it worse is that they really think what they're doing is right. You can't argue with complete and total institutional thinking."

I shook my head. "He understood exactly what I was doing. He just thought it was silly. I could tell."

"Ever read *1984,* by George Orwell?"

"Yes, and I told you I'm not a revolutionary."

"It's my favorite book. The only problem is that he didn't explain *how* the world ended up that way. That book was called *1983.*"

I knew there was no *1983.* "How, then?"

"A million little things piled up to make a big thing. Just like today." He looked at my chest, then pointed. "You know that ID card you have around your neck?"

I looked down at the plastic thing. "So?"

"It's not just an ID card. Not for security, anyway."

"I thought it was a dog collar."

He shook his head, serious. "There's a microchip in it."

I looked down at it again. My name, picture, ID number, and a bar code for the cafeteria were on it. "A microchip?"

"Yeah, and I'm not shitting you. They instituted it after the Trade Towers were hit. You know, the paranoia thing since Benders High has had so much trouble with terrorists roaming the halls."

"A microchip? No way."

"Yes, way. Know what it does?"

"What?"

"It gives complete access to your entire record, including local law enforcement and medical records. It also includes all of your personal files and information concerning school."

I sat there, thinking about it. "I've heard about some national ID card like that."

He nodded. "There's more. Have you ever noticed those little boxes above the doors of each class? They're transmitters. They track you. The school knows where you are at all times, and if you aren't where you're supposed to be, it sends a red flag to the office. Your schedule is plugged into the computer and if you aren't tagged within ten minutes in your class, it sends a message that you're a criminal to be hunted down and incarcerated without access to an attorney. They're in the bathrooms, in the cafeteria, the gym, everywhere. Even outside."

"No way."

"Fine, don't believe me. We were one of the first schools in the country to do it. Everybody was so happy we were one step closer to robots, the city council funded part of it."

"You sound like a conspiracy theorist."

"I'll tell you what. We'll play a game on Monday and we'll see what's conspiracy and what's not."

"And the rules of the game?"

"Simple. We trade cards next week and see what happens."

"Deal. What are you doing this weekend?"

He shrugged. "Lazing around being a slacker. You?"

I took a breath, remembering his comments about fitting in at Benders High. "Practicing for choir."

He squinted at me. "Choir?"

"Yeah. I'm in it."

"I thought you were anti-establishment."

I corrected him. "You said I was anti-establishment."

"You're a hard one to figure out, Poe Holly."

I shrugged. "Oh well."

He pondered the neighborhood for a minute. "That's not a bad thing. I just ..."

"You made assumptions about me just like all the people you have contempt for who make assumptions."

He leaned back, putting his hands over his heart. "Mortal wound. Ouch."

"Sad but true."

He sat back up. "You're right, but I never said I was any better than them."

I laughed. "You ooze contempt for people, Theo. Get off it."

"Yeah, but I have just as much contempt for myself, so it's okay." He smiled, giving me a smirk. "So there."

"Want to do something tomorrow?"

"Yeah. My parents are having a cocktail party. You're invited."

"Ooh. On the good people list already. I can't wait."

"It's like going to the zoo. Looking at the monkeys through the bars. Bring a bag of peanuts and they'll do tricks."

"You never let up, do you?"

He stood. "No. I'll come over at around five. Deal?"

"Deal."

I was in my room an hour later when Dad came in the front door. I stared at the music I'd been studying, thinking about what was going to happen. I didn't know how far I could push him, but I knew he'd probably be mad.

I waited for the sounds of his steps up the stairs, but they didn't come. I needed to learn the music, but I couldn't concentrate. Every time I looked at the sheets, fifteen seconds later I was reminding myself to study, forcing myself to focus.

I couldn't get used to this. To him. The waiting. The patience. It was like he'd handed me a platter of freedom when I got here, and now, as I sat in my room, it was almost like I wanted him to take it away. To do something. Anything besides calmly ask distant questions about philosophical aspects of why I was a loser. I wanted him to be pissed off.

I found him in the kitchen, a bag of groceries on the counter and the fridge open. He took a sack of tomatoes from the bag and put them in the vegetable bin, and even that made me edgy. Everything had to be perfect. "Why do you have to put everything where it belongs?"

He turned. "You mean the tomatoes?"

"I mean everything. Everything needs to be perfect around you."

He shrugged. "I don't think that's true."

"You're kidding, right? You scrub the grout lines with a toothbrush. You wash every dish five seconds after you use it. You alphabetically organize the magazines in the den. You iron your jeans. You leave for work at the exact same time every morning. To the minute. It's driving me crazy."

"What is?"

"Dad, when you slice carrots, they have to be the same size. I've seen you. You throw away the ones that aren't right."

He looked out the back window, then nodded. "Perhaps I am that way."

"Understatement of the year. Don't you ever get mad? Don't you ever throw things or leave messes or get drunk or do anything that says you're a human being?"

He looked at me. "What are you getting at, Poe?"

"I'm getting at you not getting pissed in Mr. Avery's office today. Or now. It was like you weren't even there. Just . . . nothing. You aren't even mad about it, are you?"

He shook his head. "No, I'm not."

"Why not?"

He took a breath, then exhaled. "I'm not your mother, Poe. We're different people."

"I know you're not my mother, but I guess it would be nice to know that you're somebody. I mean, it's like you don't even . . ." I shook my head and looked away.

He folded his arms. "Please, go on. It's like I don't what?"

"No. If you don't care, I don't care, and I can go talk to a plant if I want to."

"I do care."

"About what? You say you're not mad about what I did today, but I didn't see you defend me in his office. It's like you actually did just happen to be in there. Like you were a lamp or something." I rolled my eyes. "Dad the lamp."

"What would you like me to do?"

I sighed, frustrated. It was like talking to a gallon of homogenized milk. "Never mind. I'm going out."

"Okay."

I turned to leave, stared at the front door down the hall, then turned around again. "See, that's it! Okay? You say okay?" I yelled at him. "What does that mean? Where's the, 'No, you can't,' or, 'Where are you going?' or, 'Be back by ten,' or, 'Call me so I know where you are'? It's like the world just slides right on by with you standing on the outside looking in!"

He stood there looking at me like I was an alien. Like he'd just listened to a diatribe in a language he didn't understand. "Am I supposed to say those things?"

I realized then that he *really* didn't get it. It wasn't that he didn't care, he was just a complete and total social idiot. No wonder Mom left him. "No, you're supposed to tell me to go out and do whatever I want. To get high and have sex and drive drunk and hang out with convicted felons. Sorry, I got it all wrong."

"I trust you."

"You don't even KNOW me!"

"I feel that I do know you, Poe. Or at least that I'm getting to know you."

"Well, you don't, and I'm starting to think you don't know how to know anybody." I grunted. "It's not like you were around anyway, huddled away in your perfect little house for sixteen years while I wondered where the fuck my dad was."

His cheeks pooched out as he exhaled. "Now you just want to hurt me."

"What? You don't like the truth? That's what it is, DAVID! You ignore everything that's not perfect, don't you?"

"I think you behaved improperly today."

I rolled my eyes. "Well, that's a start, counselor. Any other mind-bending revelations for me?"

"I don't know that you're in the mood to talk about this."

"*I* was talking. You were standing there being a lamp again."

His eyes sharpened. "Don't mock me."

I leveled a wicked flat stare at him. "Or what?"

He looked away, flustered. "I don't see that baiting me will solve this. If you want to talk in a constructive, adult manner, I'm willing. But I'm not going to fight with you."

I stomped my foot. "I'M NOT AN ADULT! You sat there

in that office and didn't say a word! Like you totally forgot that we talked about that kind of crap the other night!"

"I was letting you handle the situation."

"Yeah. Just like you let Mom handle the situation." I crossed my arms. "Maybe she was right, you know? Maybe you just don't have the fucking courage to stand up for anything."

He shook his head. "You're diverting, Poe. This doesn't have anything to do with your mother or why we split. It's about you questioning the rules. And your language doesn't solve anything, either. We can have a civilized conversation about this without profanity."

"FUCK FUCK FUCK!" I screamed.

He turned away, looking across the room. "I think a cooldown period would be best right now."

That capped it for me. "WHY? So you can figure out how to hide how you feel? So you can figure out how to pretend everything is perfect? Fuck you."

"I'm not hiding anything, but I'm not here to antagonize the circumstance, either. Please stop swearing."

"Why are you here, then?"

He faltered. "I . . ."

"You don't know, do you?"

"I'm here to talk about what is bothering you."

"God, you *are* nothing! Just an invisible nothing!"

I saw something turn in his eyes then. Something good. Something angry. He set his jaw. "What would you have me do? Tell you that you were immature and childish today? Tell you that when your goal now is to simply hurt and destroy and bully, it reminds me of your mother? This is why I left, Poe! THIS!"

Silence for a moment, dead and still as a corpse. I looked at him. "Maybe she went insane with you because you're too chickenshit to stand up for yourself. And maybe now I understand why there was no way you could be with Mom. Or anybody." My eyes seared into his, and I couldn't stop myself. Something in me wanted this to go on, because I was disgusted. But he was right. I was just like my mom. Search and destroy. Find the weakness and rip it to shreds.

So I left.

Chapter Thirteen

Saturday rolled around with the melancholy of bad relations in the house. After our one-sided fight, I had walked around Benders Hollow six times in four hours. I hated this place. I wanted Los Angeles. I never wanted to know him again.

David avoided me, spending all day doing yard work. I watched Velveeta shoot things with a paintball gun, pretending trees and rocks and plants were God knew what prey, then watched David pick weeds. I didn't understand him, and thinking about our argument the night before, I didn't even understand me. I'd used him as a punching bag, but the more I thought about it, the more I knew that sometimes people needed to be punching bags. Just like Velveeta.

I don't know what I was so cranked up about. It *was* like he was a lamp, and every time you tried to get close to him, he turned his little switch off and used fancy say-nothing talk to keep himself apart from things. To be on the outside. That's what I didn't like. He could talk about feelings and the truth and getting to know each other until he was blue in the face, but the second you wanted to get personal, he couldn't handle it. He'd sat in that office like I was a stranger.

I thought about our first conversation after I got here. The one about what we saw in each other, and knew it was the truth. His language was just like the school. Distant and impersonal, like an analysis, and I didn't know what to do.

So I called Mom. Mistake. Deep in the jungle somewhere in South America, she'd told me to call only for emergencies. She had some sort of GPS super-duty military cell phone that got reception anywhere, but it cost something like ten bucks a minute to talk. Ninety grand for a Mercedes, okay, a hundred bucks for a phone call from your daughter, not okay.

"Hello?"

"Hi, Mom."

Static on the line. "What's wrong? Are you okay? Poe, are you okay?"

"Yeah. Just calling."

"Poe, what's wrong?"

I wanted to say my dad was impossible and that I wanted to go home. I wanted to tell her to come home. I wanted, of all things, to tell my mom she wasn't that bad. "How's the jungle?"

"Poe, I told you this line is for emergencies. I thought we talked about this? I go to the city every week and check my e-mail. You haven't even sent one, by the way, and I was disappointed."

She hadn't sent one, either. "Oh."

"Listen, I have an emergency appendectomy in five minutes. I'm going to be late, and I can't have this young woman burst on me."

"Sorry."

Her tone softened. "How are things? Good? Your father?"

"Yeah. Great."

"Good, good. I knew things would go well. Gotta run. Bye."

"Bye."

So much for that.

● ● ●

At five-fifteen, Theo skated down the street to pick me up for the cocktail party, and I waved through the window. David was on his hands and knees at the sidewalk digging dirt out of the cracks with a butter knife. He'd told me it keeps the weeds away. When I told him to squirt gas in them and light a match, he thought I was joking. I wasn't.

I hopped down the steps and met them. David stood, brushing his hands on a handkerchief, and they shook hands. "Going out for the evening, Poe?"

I nodded, indifferent. "Yeah."

He hesitated. "Where?"

"Theo's house."

Theo smiled. "Probably dinner, too, Mr. Holly."

Dad nodded. "Very well." He stood there awkwardly for a second, then cleared his throat and met my eyes. "Be home by nine, Poe."

I searched his eyes, and there was an edge in them. "Sure."

"Bye," he said, then bent down to the sidewalk.

At the corner, Theo shook his head. "What was that all about?"

"What?"

"Your dad. The way he ... I don't know. It was just weird."

I smiled. "We got in a fight last night."

"About what?"

I chuckled. "How to be a dad."

. . .

We walked the mile to Theo's house. On the other side of town and near the outskirts, his family had several acres of land and a fountain outside the circular driveway. The whole place had a rich but ranchy feel to it, like the mansion on that old eighties show *Dallas,* with J. R. Ewing and his stupid cowboy hat. The house was huge, with double doors leading into an entryway as big as our living room. Theo walked in, stopped, and spread his hands out. "Welcome to Rancho Happy Happy. If there's anything you need, click your heels three times and a neurotic and totally high fairy godmother will appear to do your bidding."

"She can't be that bad."

"She still cuts the crusts off my sandwiches."

"Oh."

"Yeah, that bad. Follow me." Theo led me through the guts of the house, and we came to the kitchen. Platters of snacks and appetizers blanketed granite counters. He picked up a huge cocktail shrimp and stuffed it in his mouth. "Hungry?"

"Sure. What time does the party start?"

He looked at the clock. "People should start arriving in the next few minutes. Of course, the higher your status, the later you have to be. It's a ranking system."

I picked up something green rolled in strips of tortilla and munched. "Mmm. Good."

"Rabbit meat inside."

I stopped chewing.

He laughed. "Joking. My mom got bored one year doing nothing for a living and took a cooking class. The instructor checked himself into a psychiatric ward by the time she finished, but she learned how to be a gourmet appetizer maker."

I didn't know what to expect when I met her, and I didn't know if I even wanted to, but with a half-dozen shrimp eaten and several more green rolled things gone, Theo's dad walked in. Dark eyes, black hair, and a rugged middle-aged face with jowls greeted me. He looked like he could be on *The Sopranos,* and I saw the resemblance to Theo in his eyes. Shadowed and intense.

He ambled toward me, pale and hairy legs jutting from khaki shorts and a big belly pooching out under an untucked leisure shirt. Four big rings, all gold, decorated hairy knuckled sausages as he held out his hand to me. "Hi. I'm Theo's dad. Or so they say." He smiled. "Poe, right?"

I shook his hand, automatically liking him. "Yes. Nice to meet you."

He gazed over the spread. "Looks like you two got a head start on things. Get all the good stuff before the troops arrive." He picked over the food. "Oooooh. Teriyaki meatballs." He fingered one from the Crock-Pot and popped it in his mouth, chomping away just like Theo. "So," he said, his mouth full, "how do you like our fair town?"

"I think it's nice."

He looked at Theo. "You haven't begun hanging around normal people, have you, son?"

Theo rolled his eyes and smiled. "Don't worry, Pops, she's not normal."

He eyed me. "I don't know. She sounds awfully normal to me." He jabbed a finger at me, his eyes twinkling. "You don't breathe fire or suspend yourself upside down at night to sleep, do you?"

"Sorry."

He nodded, raised his eyebrows, then ambled toward the sliding glass door to the back patio, another meatball pinched between his thick fingers. "I'll be damned. My son knowing normal people. Maybe the world isn't coming to an end."

Theo laughed. "It is, Dad. And I'm the anti-Christ. But don't worry, I put you on the good minion list with Mom. You'll be taking care of the sulfur pits."

He licked his finger. "God knows every father wants his son to be the anti-Christ." He turned around, walking back to the counter and swiping another meatball. "Man, these things are good. Best thing in the world getting your mother into that class, if I do say so myself."

Then Theo's mom clattered into the kitchen. In her late forties, she looked like any soccer mom in the country, high-lighted blond hair, fine cheekbones with a bit of age around her eyes, and a slim, toned body. She wore white capris, open-toed heels, a plum blouse, and a white summer jacket. Her gums showed when she smiled, and her voice, high and loud, echoed through the kitchen. "Oh my gosh, Theo, intro-duce me immediately to this lovely young lady." She strode forward, and she did have a circus smile. It was huge. She held her hand out, and as Theo introduced us, I shook it.

I realized I didn't know their last name. Here I was on the verge of dating a guy and I didn't know his last name. "Nice to meet you, ma'am."

"My pleasure, Poe. I'm so happy you came." She looked at me. "I LOVE your top! Where did you get it?"

"The Salvation Army in Anaheim."

It didn't register with her. She turned to Theo's dad. "Honey, next time we're down south, we've just got to stop by and get one." She turned back to me. "Do they stock them regularly?"

I glanced at Theo, then shook my head. "They're used, ma'am. It just depends on who brings stuff in."

She spun, twirled her finger, and opened the refrigerator. "Well, let's just hope then that somebody brings one in." With that, she brought out a bag of shrimp and replaced the ones Theo had eaten. She pointed to my top. "What do those letters mean?"

I looked down at my top, which was basically a glorified pink T-shirt with three letters scrawled in fancy, Victorian handwriting across the front. I gave Theo a panicked glance. "*FTW?* Um—"

Theo cut in. "Fuck the World."

She busied herself with replacing the green rolled things I'd eaten, smiling wider than ever. "Very nice. Very nice. A statement of sorts." She glanced at her watch. "Oh, they'll be here soon. Honey? The patio bar? Make sure there's ice?"

Theo's dad made a beeline for the sliding door and Theo hopped from his barstool. "Hey, Ma, we're going to my room. If you need us, we'll probably be naked, so knock first."

She stacked cocktail glasses on the counter. "Safe sex, Theo. Remember that. We don't want any nasty nasties, now, do we?" I cringed, and she turned to me. "You two have a good time, and make yourself at home, Poe. Come on down and mingle if you'd like. Lots of treats."

I nodded, and Theo led me out and up the stairs. He chuckled. "I told you so."

"Holy moly."

"You can say anything and she's unfazed."

Up the stairs and to the right, Theo led me down a wide hall, then opened a door. "My kingdom. Welcome."

I walked in. Black. All black. The walls were painted black and covered with eighties rock posters, a neon beer sign hung over the windows looking out on the backyard, and it was a mess. Clothes and shoes layered the floor, empty pop cans were scattered over his nightstand, dresser, and windowsill, and papers covered his computer desk. He grabbed a remote and switched on the stereo sitting next to the television. "The Number of the Beast," by Iron Maiden, piped through the surround sound. I plopped on his bed. "Nice room."

"Yeah. I don't allow the housekeeper in. She'd probably steal my stuff."

"Your stuff?"

"Yeah. Mary Jooo Wanna."

"I didn't know you smoked."

He shrugged. "Not a lot, but sometimes I have to."

"You have to?"

"Mom. She gets crazy sometimes. Like not-joking-around crazy."

"Oh."

"Wanna toke? I got some good stuff a couple weeks ago."

I shook my head. "No."

"Angel girl."

"I don't like how it makes me feel. Had a bad trip once, so I stay away."

"Fine by me." He looked out the window to the back-yard. "The horde is arriving."

I stood, walking to the window. Five or six people dressed like they were related milled around the outside bar. A pool glistened blue in the sun, and a built-in hot tub connected to it lay still as a mirror. "Nice."

"Come on, I want to show you something."

Down the stairs and to the far end of the house we went, and Theo opened a hall door. More stairs down. "What is this?"

He flicked the light on. "Basement. Where we store the bodies."

"Cool." I followed him down, and after we passed a hu-midified wine cellar with a glass door on it, he stopped at another door. I looked around. The ceilings were high, the basement deep, and half of it was unfinished. "What?"

He opened the door. "Come on in. You'll like it."

I walked in and stared. Mikes and amps and mixers and a dubbing machine, the whole nine yards. Cords lay strewn across the concrete floor, and a drum set stood in the cor-ner. It was a full-on recording studio. "No way."

"Way."

I walked further in, checking things out. State of the art. Thousands of dollars. "I didn't know you were into this, Theo."

"I'm not. The drum set is mine, but the rest is my mom's."

I furrowed my brow.

"Yeah. Before the cooking thing, it was the music thing.

She watched the first year of *American Idol* and decided she wanted to be famous."

"Wow."

He laughed. "She hasn't used it in two years. A twenty-thousand-dollar recording museum." He walked over and flipped a switch. The buzz of amps lit my ears, and the mixing board lit up. "You said you were in choir."

I stepped toward the microphone. "Yeah."

"And you were in a punk band in LA, right?"

"Yeah."

He walked over to the drums, adjusted the mike, and sat down, picking up a pair of sticks and twirling them. "You play guitar?"

"Some rhythm."

He pointed to a case in the corner. "Strap on and plug in, baby. Let's see what you got."

I laughed. "Theo . . ."

"Go. I want to hear it." He tapped the cymbal.

I clicked open the guitar case. A Fender. "How 'bout we see if you can keep up?"

He laughed. "How 'bout."

I took a minute to tune, then plug in, plucking and tweaking until I found the sound I wanted. Heavy and distorted. "You can follow?"

He nodded. "Three years of the best drum instruction money can buy. Go ahead."

I did. I ripped out a chord progression, adjusted the tone on the amp, and faced him. "Pick it up after the first progression and we'll ease into it."

I began. The song was an original, and as the staccato of the guitar ripped through the room, I felt it rise in me. The power. The song was called "Machine-Gun Love," and I'd written it myself. Fast, heavy, and totally punked, my fingers flew through the chords. Theo stared at me like I was crazy. I stopped playing. "Something wrong?"

"Holy shit, Poe. Ease into it? You don't ease into that."

I rolled my eyes and smiled. "Would an Elton John song be better?"

He growled. "Fine. Get into it and I'll pick up. I'm rusty, though, so don't say anything."

I started again, my fingers warmed up, and I nailed it head-on, pounding the chords out rapid-fire. It wasn't called "Machine-Gun Love" for nothing. Theo snagged up a couple of times on the bass drum, but he kept up. I smiled as I played, nodding the count for the lyrics, then leaning into the mike and belting out the first lines. The drums stopped again. Silence filled the room as I looked at him. "What now?"

"What now? God, Poe. You can sing. I mean sing, sing. I've never heard a punk song with a voice. Crap, no wonder you're in choir. You should be the lead soloist."

I smiled. "I am."

He gaped. "Anna Conrad?"

I gave him a sly look. "Not anymore."

He pursed his lips. "And so the real reason comes out."

"What real reason?"

"Why you joined the choir."

I shrugged. "I like singing."

"No way. You joined to beat her out. Vengeance is mine, so sayeth the friend of Velveeta."

I chuckled. "Maybe, maybe not. You'll never know."

"And so the Poe mystery deepens."

"Mystery?"

"Yeah. Half the school is wondering what your deal is."

"Then half the school can wonder. Are we going to play or sit here gossiping?"

He nodded. "I'll pick you up. Go."

And so we did. We played for over an hour, cranking the volume up until the door to the studio opened. Theo's dad stood there with several partygoers behind him. Theo smiled. "Too loud, Dad?"

He walked in, followed by the guests, all of whom had drinks in their hands. "Well, being that we got a call from two counties over, it might be considered loud."

"Sorry."

He shook his head. "That's not why we're here." He looked at me. The last song we'd played was an old ballad by Motley Crüe. "We came down to see you."

I unslung the guitar. "Me?"

"You are the person connected to the voice, I assume. Unless my son has been castrated."

I don't blush, but I blushed. "I guess so."

One of the guests stepped forward, a middle-aged guy in a baby blue polo shirt and white shorts. "Incredible. Incredible voice."

Theo's dad stepped forward. "Poe, this is my good friend Bill Conrad. His daughter sings."

Anna Conrad's father, unless this tiny town had more than one Conrad family. I shook his hand. "Nice to meet you."

"Yes." He paused. "My daughter is the lead soloist for the Elite Choir. Anna. Have you met her?"

I slid a glance to Theo, then nodded. "Yes. Sort of."

Mr. Conrad smiled. "She's actually quite a singer herself. You two should get together sometime. She might show you a trick or two. She's a great girl."

"I'm sure she is, sir."

He raised an eyebrow to me. "Have you spoken to Mrs. Baird, the choir director? The tryouts are already over, of course, but I'm sure she could make room for such an outstanding voice." He winked. "I could probably even put in a good word for you. Get you into the main chorus, probably even in the Elite Choir with that voice." He went on, enchanted with his own voice. "Who trained you?"

I smiled. "Sid."

He took a sip of his drink. "Sid? Do I know him? I'm pretty familiar with most of the top vocal trainers in the state, and I know you're from Los Angeles. Is he based out of that area?"

"He's dead."

He furrowed his brow, confused.

"Drug overdose."

"Sid who?"

"Vicious."

Theo grinned conspiratorially, but Mr. Conrad went on, scratching his head. "Sid Vicious." He waggled his finger. "You know, I think I've heard that name. Yes. I didn't know he'd died. He was very well known, wasn't he?"

I nodded. "Sort of. At least in some circles."

He smiled sadly. "Well, my condolences. If you've a need for a new trainer, Anna can give you her teacher's number and I'll put in a word for you."

"Thanks, but I think I'm fine."

After they'd gone, Theo and I stared at each other, then

busted up laughing. He set his sticks down. "You never know, Poe. He might have heard of Sid Vicious. The Sex Pistols were pretty popular with the upper-crust-attorney demographic back in the seventies."

I laughed. "Maybe."

"You are a heartless person. That poor man is going to drop Sid Vicious's name every chance he gets. You know that, don't you?"

"I don't like name-droppers, and besides, it's not my problem. He did teach me to sing. At least punk. I listened to them for like a zillion hours the first time I got a Pistols CD."

He walked around the drum set, and by the look in his eyes, I knew what he was going to do. I stood there with the guitar in my hand and watched him. He stopped in front of me, sighing. "If you're going to kiss me right now, you've got to know that I will not be a groupie. I'm not a rag doll to play with and discard once you're done having your fun."

I smiled. "Me, kiss you?"

"Yeah, like this." He leaned forward, and his lips were on mine. A second later, he withdrew. I licked my lips, the touch of him still on me.

"That was a lame kiss, groupie. I expect more from my fans." Then I leaned forward, and we were blissfully sucking face with a Fender Stratocaster between us. If there was a heaven, I was in it. His hands went to my hips and he moved closer, his fingers roaming up my waist. Too high. I backed away. "Whoa. Slow down there, cowboy. I'm not a slut."

He sighed. "Dang, I was hoping you were. I go after all the sluts."

"Ha ha. I don't even know your last name."

"Dorr."

I stared at him. "Dorr? You're kidding, right?"

"No. You met my mom."

"Yeah, but Theo Dorr?"

He nodded. "She thought it would be cute to subject me to never-ending ridicule and humiliation."

I laughed. "Theo Dorr. Is your full name Theodore Dorr?"

"No, just Theo. Theo Dorr at your service. And if you don't stop making fun of me, I'll play Yellow Pages man again. Let my fingers do the walking."

"And I'll play bust your head open with this guitar."

He shrugged, glancing at my boobs. "They're nice."

I played the first few chords of "Love Stinks," and he got the picture. I sat on a stool. "So, what's going to happen with this whole Anna thing? Her dad obviously doesn't know what's going on, and practice is Monday morning."

"Couldn't tell ya. Anna's not that bad, though."

I rolled my eyes. "Yeah, even though she writes love letters to dorks so they get harassed and abused by her buddies."

He looked away. "I've known her ever since she was in first grade."

I stared at him. "Don't even tell me . . ."

"Oh God, here it comes." He stuffed his hands in his pockets. "Yes, I was infatuated with her all through junior high."

I laughed. "You and her? Oh my God, Theo."

"Hey, she is hot, and before she got a stick wedged up her ass, she was nice. You've got to understand that there is a mentality around here. Even if I'm on the outside, all the townies stick together."

I rolled my eyes again. "And so the tribe has spoken. Is this going to cause a problem with her?"

"This?"

"Us."

"We're an us?"

"Well, you did just kiss me, and I don't kiss boys unless I'm dating them."

He smiled. "No problem. She hasn't spoken a word to me in two years."

"Did you date?"

"Not even. I don't rise to the social caliber she needs to maintain her reputation."

"Oh, a bitter love, then."

"A little bit, but nothing I can't handle. And I wouldn't call it love anyway. I just wanted to have sex with her because she was the first seventh grader to get boobs."

I smirked. "Typical male."

He smiled. "Totally, and thank you very much. I pride myself on liking boobs."

"So I'm dating a male chauvinist pig. Great."

"No, you're dating a guy who likes boobs. I can't help it, and besides that, I don't think you'd like to date a guy who liked penises."

I laughed. "True enough."

"Actually, you're my first, uh, significant other unless you count Kathy Bean in second grade."

"Really? She was your first girl, huh?"

"Yeah. She didn't like Tater Tots and I did, so she let me have hers."

"Romantic."

"I thought it was grounds for dating. Still do, as a matter of fact."

"Well, you can have my Tater Tots."

He shrugged. "I already tried."

"Not those, jerk."

He laughed. "Sorry. The opportunity arose."

Chapter Fourteen

A sprinkle of rain misted my head and shoulders Monday morning as I walked to school early. Choir practice. The big announcement. Vengeance on Anna Conrad dissolved as I walked, replaced with nervous anticipation. I hate the unknown, and just as Anna left my mind, the thought of walking into that room entered, leaving me feeling like a little girl on her way to the first day of kindergarten. I hoped Mrs. Baird would keep it low-key. No gala celebration for the new kid on the block, but a quick and easy slide in.

I almost hoped Mrs. Baird would take Anna aside to explain. Tell her in private, at least. Call it a moment of guilt or stupidity, but there were boundaries of evil I wasn't willing to cross, and Anna didn't deserve total and complete humiliation. As I entered the music building, I decided human empathy sucked. I was supposed to march in that room without an ounce of remorse and with a heaping plate of spite, but I couldn't bring myself to do it. Easy to think, hard to do when it comes down to it. I thought of Theo saying she wasn't that bad, then thought about how I felt when things like that happened to me. The sinking pit of doom in my stomach. The urge to melt to the floor and ooze through the cracks.

I almost didn't want to go in, but then I remembered: I was walking into a room to take the place of the lead vocalist for an award-winning choir based on nothing but talent.

As I entered, groups and clusters of kids lounged around waiting for practice to begin. I recognized some from my classes, even got a few smiles and nods, but most I didn't know. Then I saw Anna Conrad. The glance she gave me didn't speak of anything. Neutral compared to the surprised distaste in the look of the three girls with her. I guessed they were the other soloists. The Elite Choir was called that for a reason, it seems.

I set my bag down and took a seat, waiting. Six or eight stragglers came in after me, then Mrs. Baird walked in. She set a stack of files down and faced us. "Good morning, everybody. A gloomy day, but a good one to be inside and singing. Welcome." She stepped forward, glancing at me before going on. "We have a new member and I'd like to introduce Poe Holly to you. My hope is that you'll welcome her with open arms and warmth. She's a fantastic singer, and one that will be a great addition to our group." With that, she swept her arm to me.

I didn't stand but nodded, and thank God above Mrs. Baird went on. "Everybody, please take your positions on the stage and we'll get started." Students filed onto the stage. Tiered platforms arced around the stage in a slight curve, and I stayed put, not knowing where to go. My eyes fell on Anna and the three girls she'd been talking to. She and two of the girls stepped to a separate area in the center of the stage. The soloist positions. I stood, walking toward them.

Mrs. Baird glanced at them, then cleared her throat. I slowed. She spoke as she pointed. "Poe, if you'd like to take your place to the left of Angela, we'll begin."

I looked at Mrs. Baird. "I don't know who . . ."

"Angela, please raise your hand."

Angela raised her hand and smiled. From the second row of the main chorus singers. I faltered, staring at Mrs. Baird. She ignored me. The pit of doom in my stomach swooped in. My mouth went dry. The entire choir faced me, and I couldn't do anything. Every feeling I'd had about Anna Conrad came back to me. Now it was me, not her. I took my place.

One hour of me being too chicken to walk out of the room later had me and the rest of the chorus packing up our bags to head for regular classes. Mrs. Baird called me aside as the others left. I stood in front of her, a picture of serenity and peace covering a nuclear holocaust ready to explode. I said nothing. Mrs. Baird blinked, then cleared her throat. "You're probably wondering . . ."

"I'm not wondering."

She looked at me. "When I spoke to Anna Conrad's parents about placing you as the lead soloist, they . . ."

"I said I'm not wondering."

She sighed. "Poe . . ."

"What?"

"I'm sorry."

I laughed, the sting of the knife in my back. "Sorry. Really? Gosh, let's throw a pity party for Poe because she got the shaft from a liar."

Her eye twitched, and she put her hand on her desk. "When I told you I could put you on as the lead soloist, I spoke out of turn. There are other things at play here, and I apologize for that. But there is no reason to be confrontational here, and there's no reason for name-calling."

I smiled wickedly. "I'm sorry, but I see a liar in front of me, and if you go look in a mirror, you will, too. Just calling it like I see it, Mrs. Baird. No politics involved, right? Just the truth."

Her eyes narrowed. "That's enough."

"Or what? You'll stab me in the back because Anna Conrad's parents pull your strings?" I rolled my eyes.

She shook her head. "Anna's parents don't pull my strings."

"God, do you ever listen to yourself?"

"Excuse me?"

I laughed. "You sound like a complete idiot. Weak." I turned and walked to the door, then turned back around, the anger spilling out. I raised my voice. "You and I both know the only reason I'm not in the soloist group is that once Anna's parents found out about it, they made calls." I shook my head. "I bet you got all three soloists' parents barking in your ear, huh? Then maybe the vice principal? Somebody from the district? Maybe they looked at my transcripts? My discipline report?"

She said nothing but shuffled, crossing her arms over her chest. .

"That's what I thought. Can't have the trash front and center, now, can you? Talent my ass, lady. You suck."

A pained expression came to her face, and I could tell she was sincere with it. "Poe, I can't—"

121

I interrupted her. "Can you answer one question for me, please?"

She closed her mouth, stared at me, then nodded.

"Do you enjoy being owned?" Then I turned and walked out.

Chapter Fifteen

Anna Conrad waited for me outside the choir room. She'd heard the whole thing. I didn't even want to look at her. I thought about the party where her dad had smiled and winked at me about getting in the chorus, and I knew that he'd known. The joke was on me. I walked past her. Her voice rang out. "I don't agree."

I stopped, turning around. "It would be a good thing to stay away from me."

She inhaled, then let the breath out. "I know what happened."

"Good for you. Maybe you could tell all your friends, too. I'm sure they'd get a kick out of it."

She shook her head. "I haven't told anybody."

I walked up to her. Velveeta flooded my mind. "Why'd you do it?"

She furrowed her brow. "What?"

"Velveeta. Why'd you write that letter?"

She blinked, caught by surprise. "I didn't know. . . ." She sighed. "I didn't know they were going to do that. I thought it was just fun. Just teasing him a little."

My hand swung in an arc, a flash of pale, and I slapped her. Hard. The sound echoed down the empty hall as she reeled and let out a squeal of pain. She came up with her hand on her face, defensive and waiting for me to attack. Blood seeped down her lip, and tears gathered in her eyes. As she licked the crimson from her mouth, a momentary flash of sickness went through me as I remembered Velveeta's battered face. But I stepped toward her, my eyes drilling hers. "Bitch." Then I turned and walked away.

Theo met me at my locker before first period, all smiles compared to the thunderclouds over my head. His grin faltered, and he stopped short. "What's wrong?"

"Nothing. Bad day." I grabbed my books and closed the locker.

He walked with me. "Ready?"

"For what? Armageddon?"

He laughed. "Man, you are in a bad mood. What happened?"

"Nothing. What should I be ready for?"

"Trading ID cards. Remember?"

The last thing I wanted to do was even be here, but I'd checked out the little black boxes placed everywhere, and I still didn't believe him. I took mine off. "Here."

We traded, and he put mine on. "We'll meet here after first period and trade back."

"What's going to happen?"

"They'll call you to the office and ask why you were in the wrong place. No biggie, really."

First and second periods slogged by with nothing for me to do but think about choir, Mrs. Baird, slapping Anna Conrad, and what would happen because of it. Theo and I traded back our ID cards after first period, and just before class let out second period, I got the call to the office like he said I would.

As I walked in the administration building, Theo stood at the counter, smiling at me. Ms. Appleway sat behind the counter dutifully ignoring Theo. I joined him. "You were right."

He smiled. "Told ya."

Ms. Appleway looked up. "Okay, you two. What's going on?"

Theo gave her a wide-eyed look of innocence. "Were all the sheep not in the pens, Ms. Appleway?"

She narrowed her eyes. "No, they weren't, Mr. Dorr. And don't pull any of your funny stuff on me. Cough up your excuse and get to class."

He smiled. "Have I ever told you that I find older women incredibly attractive, Ms. Appleway? I simply wanted to be in your presence."

She smiled, a twinkle in her eye. "I've half a mind to put you across my knee with a paddle to your butt."

He sighed. "Okay, fine. Poe and I switched cards so I could prove to her that we're nothing more than inhuman bytes of information tracked by the evil big brother. She didn't believe me when I told her that we're heading toward a wonderful brave new world and that if a glitch in our productivity levels showed up, we would be sent here for social reconditioning."

She looked to the counter, writing out passes. "That I won't argue, Mr. Dorr, but perhaps you should think twice about getting your friend here in trouble to prove a point. I'll be speaking to both your parents this afternoon."

Theo took his pass when she handed it to him. "Trouble is the only trait that separates us from the milky-eyed masses, Ms. Appleway. I cannot give up my humanity quite yet. At least not until KISS does another reunion tour. I missed the first one."

"Go away, revolutionary upstart." She looked at me. "You do know what you're getting yourself into with this boy, right?"

I nodded, smiling as I took my pass. "I've been warned."

Theo and I walked to third-hour current affairs, and when we came in, Mr. Halvorson, chief executive president and dictator of the Equality Club, gave us a smirk when we handed him our passes. "Take your seats."

We did, and then listened to a thirty-minute monologue on the important economic relationships we had with several Middle Eastern countries, with Mr. Halvorson blithely leaving out the fact that it was still okay in most places to stone women to death for being women. When I brought up the fact that women had less standing than lizards in some of our "partner" cultures, he dutifully told the class that it's not our place to judge, it's our place to respect diversity.

He didn't like it when I told him political correctness and oil prices mixed well and that female genital mutilation had always been something I'd like to explore.

After class, Theo and I parted ways, and I headed for the gym. PE. Great. Another Poe defeat waiting to greet me with my shitty PE shirt. This day couldn't get any worse. In the locker room, I opened my bag and saw my choir gown, still in the plastic wrapper, stuffed at the bottom. I wouldn't be needing that anymore, I thought, ditching my boots and putting my sweats on. Then I stopped.

A grin split my face as I stared at my pack. Fine. They wanted to play games, I'd play the game. Mrs. Baird and Vice Principal Avery could stuff it where the sun didn't shine. I took the gown from the wrapper, unfolded it, looked at the Benders High emblem on it, then put it on.

Several girls walked by, staring at me standing in the gym locker room wearing a choir gown, and I couldn't care less. I couldn't care less about anybody in this stinking place. I stowed my stuff in my locker and walked into the gym. Just as I entered, Coach Policheck blew her whistle for us to line up. Everybody stared at me, and laughter rose. I took my place in line.

Coach Policheck looked at me, shook her head, then trudged over. "One chance, Poe. Change it or go to the office immediately."

I stood silent.

She pointed to the doors. "Go."

I left.

I wore my gown to the office. Ms. Appleway smiled. "Twice in one day, Poe. Mr. Avery is waiting."

I walked into his office, and he sat behind his desk, the huge girth of his belly touching the edge of the wood surface. He glanced at me, then down at my file, then motioned for me to take a seat. I did. He looked up, sighed, then deflated, leaning his elbows on the desk. "Well, Ms. Holly, I don't know what to do with you."

I stared at him, sick of everything. "Maybe you should find somebody that does."

He looked at my choir gown. "You know this is ridiculous."

"No, it's not."

127

His face hardened. "You cannot wear your choir gown to PE. We talked about this last week."

"You told me that as long as you had an official Benders High uniform, you had a choice. It's a uniform with the insignia. I'm following your rules."

"You *cannot* wear it." With that, he picked up his phone and punched an extension. "Yes, David. Would you please come to my office? Your daughter is here. Yes, she is. Again."

Dad came in a moment later, looked at me, then took a seat. I turned to Mr. Avery. "Cool, the lamp is here."

Confusion clouded Mr. Avery's face, but he let it pass. "David, Poe has decided to construe my words the other day as it being okay to wear her choir gown to PE."

Dad looked at me, then at Mr. Avery, taking a moment. "Construe?"

"Yes. She's not being reasonable about this, and I can't stand for making a scene simply because she doesn't like the rules."

Dad shook his head. "I don't agree."

Mr. Avery blinked. "I'm sorry?"

He glanced at me and a flicker of a smile, nervous and sad at the same time, came over his face. "You stipulated the rules the other day to Poe."

He scoffed. "David, come on. We can't have disorder like this. She's making a mockery of this school. She knows exactly what I was talking about last week. Sports uniforms. Not choir uniforms. She's causing trouble for the sake of trouble."

Dad coughed and took on a serious tone. "Poe is proving a point, and I agree with it. The policy is inherently unfair to the students who do not or cannot play sports," he said, meeting Mr. Avery's stare with a shrug. "It gives some students a choice where other students have none, Steve, and it serves no practical purpose other than to create exactly what we supposedly stand against at this school. Favoritism and class-based discrimination. If choice is to be given, it should be given to the whole, not the part."

Mr. Avery flipped his pen on the desk, frustrated. "What would you have me do, then? Change the policy? We've always done it that way and it's never been a problem. It's trivial."

I rolled my eyes. "The only reason it's trivial is that you don't have to do it."

Mr. Avery stared at me. "Okay, if you were in my position, what would you do? Have everybody wear the same uniform, right?"

"Get rid of the whole uniform rule in the first place." I smirked. "Everybody knows who the special people are anyway, and I'm sure you can think of other ways to put us losers down."

He shook his head. "First of all, Poe, you are not a loser, and there are no 'special people' at this school. We're all equal here."

I laughed. "The choir and the football team are the prancing fairies of this rat hole."

He sat back again, at his wits' end. "You *are* part of the choir! What more do you want?"

I looked at him, the door wide open for Poe the Destructor to come barging through. "Yeah, the choir. You'd know all about that, huh, Mr. Avery?"

Dad furrowed his brow. "What?"

I smiled at Mr. Avery. "Nothing, Dad. I'm sure Mr. Avery has no idea that after Anna Conrad's parents complained, I was booted from the lead soloist's spot. I don't quite 'fit' into it as well as Anna. Right, Mr. Avery?"

He blustered, and I knew he knew. How much he had to do with it was another subject, though. A dim lightbulb lit above his head. "I see this situation has to do with more than just PE."

"They're pretty much the same."

Dad frowned, interrupting. "What happened in choir?"

"I won the lead solo spot, but Benders High School decided I shouldn't have it."

Mr. Avery shook his head. "No, no. That's not what happened. You missed tryouts, and the rule says you have to try out. When that was brought to Mrs. Baird's attention, she had to comply. There was no favoritism."

I stared at him like he was a dead fish. "Then why am I in the Elite Choir at all? You just said you have to try out. Even for a regular spot, right? Well, according to you, I shouldn't be in the choir at all."

"Well..."

"Oh, I get it. Sometimes the rules apply and sometimes they don't. It just depends on who, right? Just like PE?"

"No, that's not it."

I laughed, triumphant. "Yes, it is."

Mr. Avery looked at my dad. "She was given a spot in the Elite Choir without a tryout because Mrs. Baird felt responsible for misleading Poe about being a soloist. To give her a chance."

"I don't need a chance! I did try out and I'm better than Anna!"

Dad spoke up. "I think you should answer my daughter's question, Steve. Then I think you should furnish a written copy of the rules for me." Mr. Avery blinked at my dad, but he went on, "I'm here as a father, Steve, not as an employee of this school. I'm sure you understand that."

Mr. Avery took a moment, then nodded. "Very well. There are no written rules about tryouts, David, just as there are no written rules about the allowance of football jerseys in PE."

Dad nodded. "Then why was Poe ousted?"

Mr. Avery cleared his throat, glancing at me before continuing. "Can we have a moment, David? I . . ."

Dad looked at me. "I think if you've something to say, you should say it, Steve."

He nodded. "I'm afraid there were complaints when it was found out that Anna would be bumped, and the rules were questioned."

I smirked. "So you listen to some complaints but not others? Is that in the invisible rule book, too?"

He glowered at me, so caught in his own words he couldn't get out. He took a sip of coffee, composing himself. "Poe, I think you should go back to class. I'm going to excuse today, just this one time, but you'll have to wear your uniform to PE from now on. And I expect your tone and attitude to improve, too. There's no need for nastiness. We can be civil."

"No."

Mr. Avery brought himself to bear, leaning forward over the desk. He looked toward my dad. "Listen, if we hand out special treatment to everybody who doesn't want to follow the rules, it would be chaos. Sometimes we have to sacrifice to maintain stability."

I laughed, and I laughed loud. "So I'm sacrificed to maintain stability. That's screwed in the head."

Dad glowered. "Poe . . ."

"No, I'm not getting this." I looked at Mr. Avery. "So basically you want to make sure everybody knows their place in this school, right? There's this group and that group and the other group, and the 'rules' you make up as you go along let us all know where we should be, right? At least you could admit it."

Mr. Avery sniffed. "You're twisting things around here. There's nothing wrong with individuality and distinction when you've earned it, Poe. That's what you're not understanding about the jerseys. They earned it on merit."

I crossed my arms. "I earned my choir uniform on merit."

He smirked. "But choir has nothing to do with playing Ping-Pong or tennis in PE class, Poe, it has to do with singing."

I shrugged, pondering the ceiling for a moment. "What does football have to do with playing volleyball in PE class?"

Mr. Avery blinked. "Listen, I know what you're saying, and I know what you're trying to do, but this is a waste of time. I see you as equal to anybody here."

I exploded. "Don't sit there and tell me we're all the same, because we're not! And YOU make it that way!" I sat back. "I didn't ask for any of this! You screwed me, and now I'm screwing you."

Mr. Avery almost choked he was so frustrated. "You didn't try out, Poe. You didn't follow the rules."

"Mrs. Baird TOLD me it was a tryout! You just said there were no rules! God, you're just caving in because people are breathing down your neck."

He ran his hands over his chubby cheeks, groaning. "I wasn't the one with anybody breathing down my neck, Poe." He turned to my dad. "I think the best thing to do is talk with Principal Stephens. Maybe even Superintendent Marny. I don't have the power to change this even if I wanted to, David."

Almost on the verge of tears, I clenched my teeth. "You see it, don't you, Mr. Avery? Don't you?"

He sighed. "Poe, I do see it, but this is a mess. I have a job to do, and I'm answerable to the whole school. The whole community. Not just you." He drummed his fingers on the desk, his eyes drooping. "Sometimes that's just the way the world is, Poe, and I'm sorry."

"Fine, then. I quit anyway. I never even wanted this in the first place. I never even wanted to be here."

Dad cut in. "Poe, please."

"No, Dad, don't. I'm not doing it. I tried to do it your way, and they made it clear. I quit." I picked up my bag.

He started to say something, but I walked out, slamming the door on my way. Ms. Appleway, with a pensive smile that said she'd heard me yelling, nodded as I passed. "Don't quit, girl."

Then I was gone.

Chapter Sixteen

Of all the people in the world I didn't want to see, Velveeta was one of them. I walked home, done with Benders High, done with Benders Hollow, and done with the world. Velveeta knelt on all fours in the garden, weeding the dandelions popping up here and there. His lip pooched with a wad of tobacco as he turned his head and stared at me. "Hey, Poe. You ain't in school today?"

I rolled my eyes. "I'm standing here, aren't I?"

"You sure are. I ain't in school, either."

"I guess you being here is the giveaway."

He smiled. "Had a doctor's appointment and Aunt Vicky said I could stay home the rest of the day if I weeded." He pointed. "Chores."

"What's wrong?"

"Got a boil on my back. Lanced the sucker." He stood, wiping his hands on his thighs and making a stabbing gesture. White knobby knees stained green poked out under his shorts. "Wanna see?"

"No."

He smiled. "Your loss. Like a volcano erupting. Mount

Vesuvial." He grimaced, shading his eyes from the sun. "What're you doing out?"

"I'm moving back home."

"Why?"

"I don't fit in here. And it sucks."

"That's the stupidest thing I ever heard."

I stared at him. "Why?"

He laughed, then spit a stream of brown loogey on the grass. "You don't fit in because you don't *want* to fit in, girl."

"So?"

"So, it could be different."

"How's that?"

"You could not fit in because you *can't* fit in." He smiled, a tendril of tobacco stuck to his front tooth.

"It's all the same anyway, Velveeta."

"No, it ain't. You could fit in, but you don't want to. I can't fit in because some things just aren't meant to be."

"You could fit in just like anybody else."

He made a dopey face, like I was the dope. "You get yourself a haircut, some normal clothes, and wear some pretty makeup and you could be anyone you wanted. Me? You put me in a thousand-dollar suit and you still got a dork named Velveeta. Ain't nothing changes that."

I clenched my teeth. "I didn't come over here to listen to this. Especially today. I don't need a guilt trip about how good I have it."

He frowned, then smiled. "Well, I don't want you to go."

"Why?"

135

"Because you're the only friend I got here, that's why. And besides, I didn't figure you for a faker."

"I'm not a faker."

"Are too, going home like a whipped puppy with his tail 'tween her legs."

"Don't tell me you wouldn't leave if you could."

He screwed his eyes at me, the expression constantly changing on his long, odd face. "What makes you think it would be different anywhere else I went?" He shrugged. "I'm stuck with me."

"You wish you were somebody else?"

"Half the time I wish I wasn't anything, other half I wish I could jump outta my skin and leave it in a heap on the floor."

"Pity party for Velveeta."

He knelt, digging up a weed. "Ain't nothing wrong with saying how I feel, and 'sides, you don't have to make me feel bad on account of you feeling bad." He cocked his head up at me. "Don't you have some bags to pack or something?"

I watched him root the weeds out for a minute more, thinking about what he said, then walked inside.

• • •

By the time Dad got home, I'd been lying on my bed doing absolutely nothing but thinking for three hours. I heard him down in the kitchen, no doubt organizing groceries for dinner, and padded downstairs. "Hi."

He turned. "Hi."

"I'm sorry about today."

He shook his head. "No, I'm sorry I didn't come to my senses before this."

136

I leaned against the entryway. "I'm not leaving."

He smiled, then nodded. "I figured you wouldn't."

"Why?"

"Because I know you. At least I think I do." He walked up to me, put my head in his hands, and kissed my forehead. "We'll do this together, okay?"

His eyes mirrored mine. "You could lose your job. You know that."

"We'll deal with that as it comes. I spoke to Mrs. Baird this afternoon and got pretty much the same story. I've scheduled a meeting with Superintendent Marny tomorrow and we'll lodge a formal complaint with the school board. We'll get to the bottom of this."

He turned away then, back at the counter and putting away vegetables. I watched him for a minute, not exactly knowing what to do with myself. Mom would've never done this. "No."

He turned around. "What?"

"I don't want you to do this."

"Poe . . ."

"No. It's not worth it. It is stupid, and I didn't even want to be in choir. The only reason I did was to get back at Anna Conrad."

"She's the one who wrote the letter?"

"Yes. I slapped her today. Out in the hall after practice."

"Because of Velveeta?"

"No. Yes. I don't know. Because she is who she is."

"Well, that doesn't change the fact that what's happening is wrong."

"Dad, I really want to handle this myself. I've thought

about it. That's all I've been thinking about since I got home."

He stood across the kitchen from me, and he looked alone. So alone. "Are you sure?"

I smiled. "Yeah, I'm sure."

Chapter Seventeen

Theo met me at the soda and candy machines in the main building the next morning, and as I put my coins in for my morning Mountain Dew, he pointed to the machine. "You know what that thing is, don't you?"

I looked at the dispenser. "My first assumption would be that it's probably a soda machine. I suppose it's not, though."

He narrowed his eyes, peering at it suspiciously. "Nope, it's not. Might look like a convenient bit of technology to quench the thirst for a few pennies, but it's not. It's actually a method of cradle-to-grave marketing indoctrination to continue our desire to consume properly."

"It's a soda machine."

He laughed as we passed a sign on the wall advertising candy bars. "It's target marketing. Complete inundation of a product to create and keep addicts like you within their clutches, and it's happily promoted by our public education system. You get it before school, during school, and after school now. It's inescapable."

"It's a soda machine."

"Yeah, a soda machine and advertising that our dear school receives healthy amounts of compensation for. Money. The district got together and decided they would promote adult-onset diabetes, obesity, and the leading cause of tooth decay in America. They're teaching us how to consume mass amounts of sugar through constant media indoctrination. A good lesson in my book."

I rolled my eyes. "I've seen you put money in them."

He shrugged. "Just trying to be a good student consumer."

"Where do you come up with this stuff?"

"I don't come up with anything. You see a soda machine, I see the true motivation of our public educators exposed. I added 'em up last year. There are thirty-seven corporate advertisers in this school, from the machines to class promotions to sponsored events. It's all about the money, baby, and I'm just lookin' out for you," he said, then quick as a flash, he kissed my cheek as we walked. His lips were warm. I threw my soda in the garbage at the door to the courtyard, and Theo smiled. "There's some buzz going around."

"About what?"

"Anna Conrad. It seems she was horrifically and systematically beaten on the right side of her face yesterday. The assailant is unknown."

I smiled. "My hand still aches."

He nodded. "Figured it was you."

I rolled my eyes. "So is she after me now?"

"Nope. She won't say a word about it."

"So what's the big deal?"

"Colby Morris."

"What does Colby Morris have to do with that?"

"Anna won't give up who did it. Word is Colby thinks Velveeta did it because of the note. The Golden Boy is on the hunt for the Cheese Man."

My stomach sank. "Shit. Vel wasn't even at school yesterday."

"Shit is what's going to hit the fan. My intuitive sensibilities are telling me it'll probably come down before next hour. Current affairs. If not, then after school or some other time. Did I ever tell you I'm almost psychic?"

"He didn't do it, though."

"A bloodbath awaits."

. . .

I fidgeted all through second hour, wondering what I should do. Five minutes before class let out, I excused myself to the bathroom and walked to Mr. Halvorson's class, waiting across the hall. I had to catch Velveeta before Colby got to him, but I didn't know what class Velveeta had before Halvorson's, so I was stuck.

When class let out, the halls went from dead silent and empty to a chorus of voices and bodies bumping into each other. Then I saw Vel turn the corner at the end of the hall, his head down, shoulders hunched, and his eyes at his feet, the usual way he walked anywhere.

As Velveeta passed the restroom at the corner, hands snapped out and clenched his upper arms, and the flash of two Benders High varsity jackets yanked him into the bathroom. I started, almost yelled, but shut my mouth and double-timed it down the hall.

As I neared the restroom door, a football player, a guy I'd seen around, stood next to the drinking fountain. He blocked my way as I tried to go in, smiling down at me. "Ladies' room is at the other end."

"Get out of my way."

His smile disappeared. He didn't move, just shook his head.

He wasn't expecting it, and when my knee jerked up and caught him square in the balls, he folded like a paper doll. I banged through the door, then stopped, wide-eyed. At least fifteen guys, most in varsity jackets, filled the place. With a wall of bodies in front of me, I couldn't see anything, but I could hear. I could hear Colby Morris swearing, I could hear the thud of a beating, and I could hear Velveeta.

I pushed through the smiling and laughing crowd, and as it gave way, I saw it. Velveeta curled up in a fetal position under the far sink with his arms protecting his head and Colby Morris, his hands braced on the porcelain above, kicking and stomping the living crap out of him. Over and over and over, so fast and vicious that his leg looked like a piston. Blood spattered on the tile walls and floor, and Velveeta grunted and whined with each blow.

I ran forward, screaming that he didn't do it, and two guys grabbed me, one covering my mouth with his hand. I fought and kicked and struggled but couldn't move, pinned to the wall. Colby kept kicking, his foot slamming repeatedly against Vel with sickening thuds. Colby's shoe left a bloody footprint on the tile floor as he turned, his chest heaving as he stared at me. There was no smile, no laugh, nothing but a slit of rage for a mouth and a hazy, almost trance-like look in his eyes.

Silence filled the bathroom. My eyes went to Velveeta,

but he lay unmoving. Tears streamed down my face, and I yanked away, facing Colby. "He didn't do it! I did! I slapped her!"

Chest still heaving, he glanced at Velveeta, then back to me. "So fucking what. Maybe that will teach you a lesson, bitch." He looked around at his buddies. Some looked away, others stared at Velveeta, others laughed. Colby shouldered through the crowd, and as he passed me, he slammed my chest, forcing me against the wall. "Say a word and I'll kill him."

I grimaced. "You asshol—"

His hand flashed out and he slapped me, his fingers stinging my ear. "Shut your fucking mouth." Then he stomped through the door.

By then, guys were filing out, disappearing, and none of them, not a single one, would look me in the eye. In another moment, the place was empty. The whole thing had taken less than three minutes. Velveeta lay still.

I fell to my knees, touching his shoulder and calling his name, trying to control myself, but I couldn't. I sobbed over his bloody face and he groaned, opening the eye that would open. The other eye had a deep cut above it, blood pulsing out with the beat of his heart. His nose was swollen and pouring blood, and his lips were mashed. He said nothing.

I reached up and grabbed a wad of paper towels, running them under the faucet and pressing them to his eye. He winced, groggy, and I told him it would be okay. It wasn't okay. It was so out-of-bounds I didn't know what to do with myself. This was my fault. One hundred percent my fault. Colby Morris was psychotic. Then the bathroom door opened.

Mr. Halvorson walked in, took in the scene, told me not to move him, then ran out. Two minutes later he rushed back in, told me help was on the way, and knelt beside us, taking more paper towels and scooting me out of the way. "Who did this?"

I slumped against the wall. "You know who did this. Everybody in this school knows who did this."

"Tell me."

"Colby Morris and half the football team."

Velveeta groaned, his one good eye staring me down, letting me know he'd heard what Colby said. There was a warning in that look. "I fell."

I shook my head. "It was Colby Morris. I saw it, and at least fifteen other guys saw it, too."

Chapter Eighteen

Velveeta checked out of the emergency room four hours later with nine stitches above his eye, a broken nose, a chipped tooth, and two bruised ribs. I sat with him the whole time. He looked like he'd been put through a blender.

Two cops had come in and taken a report, but Velveeta refused to say who did it or to press charges. I told them who'd done it, but they said there was nothing they could do unless the victim pressed charges. Vel wouldn't. His aunt tried, but with no result. My dad came down and tried, too, but nothing worked, and after that, Dad talked to the cops out in the hall.

As we drove home, he told me that charges could possibly be filed if the district attorney thought it worthwhile. We'd find out soon enough. I shook my head. "He's expelled, right?"

Dad sighed. "I don't know. I'm sure the school will do an investigation."

"They could start by talking to the football team."

"I know, Poe, I know." He glanced at me as we pulled in the driveway. "You might have saved his life."

"He thought Velveeta was the one who hit Anna. Because of the note."

Silence.

"It's my fault."

"It's a misunderstanding, yes, but it's not your fault. Colby Morris is responsible for this."

I couldn't help it. Tears built in my eyes. "No, it's my fault. None of this would have ever happened if I hadn't pushed it."

Silence.

"You agree, don't you?"

"There is absolutely no excuse for what happened to Velveeta, Poe. None. You made a mistake with Anna, but Colby is responsible for this."

"Then why don't I feel better about it?"

Dad put it in park. "Because you're a human being."

I got out of the car. "He's going to pay."

He looked at me. "Poe . . ."

"He is. I swear it. He'll pay."

• • •

Wednesday morning came with the revolting thought of going to school. Velveeta was on doctor's orders to stay in bed on account of a severe concussion, and I had choir practice before first hour. I didn't want to go, but I did. Business as usual, but it wasn't. It was pretend business as usual.

When I saw Anna standing with her group of friends in the choir room, my mind flipped to Velveeta curled up and bleeding under the sink. Anna looked at me for too long, no expression on her face, and I almost erupted.

Mrs. Baird came in and had us take our places, and we

began. I sang halfheartedly, staring at Anna's back with pure malice in my heart, and the anger burned. Every verse I sang, it rose, and my voice rose with it. My chest swelled as I breathed with the lines, the feeling pouring through me like a river, and I knew I was too loud for the chorus.

As Mrs. Baird directed, she kept glancing at me, trying to quiet me down, but I didn't. And when the chorus verse ended and Anna faded in for her piece, I shut my mouth. She was good. Very good. As good as they said.

I was better. So I opened my mouth.

It started quiet, but it built. Within a minute, Mrs. Baird put her hands down to signal a halt, but I kept singing. So did Anna, raising it up a notch. Mrs. Baird stared bullets into me, but I smiled, my voice catapulting over Anna's and crushing hers. If they wanted a tryout, here it was, and they could shove a big stick up their asses if they thought that Poe Holly would roll over.

After another moment, Anna stopped, her voice dwarfed by mine. I continued, finishing her piece to the absolute silence of the choir. Not a sound was made when I stopped. Mrs. Baird stared, angry. I stepped down from my spot, giving back what she gave. "I'll see you Friday morning. Seven-thirty." Then I walked out.

Colby Morris wasn't in school, and the word from Theo was that he was lying low until the school made a decision about things. Mr. Halvorson acted like he hadn't found a severely beaten and bloody outcast under the sink in the boys' bathroom, and I figured as the head of the Committee of Equality and Fairness at Benders High, he had a duty to ignore the issues that really mattered.

Theo met me after school, and we walked to my house.

Dad would be late. He was offering counseling services to those who might be affected by the beating that Colby Morris hadn't given Velveeta, and I laughed at the thought. Theo looked at me. "Inside joke?"

"My dad. He's staying late in case anybody was traumatized by the violence of what didn't happen."

"State-sponsored wussy treatment. I'm sure he's got a packed house full of traumatized teenagers."

"Yeah, right. More people would be lining up to buy a video of it than for counseling."

"Yep. I haven't heard anything."

"Colby should be expelled and arrested."

"He won't be," Theo said, his tone resigned.

We walked up to the porch and slumped in the chairs. "Tell me why not."

"His dad is an administrator for the county jail."

"So?"

"Come on, Poe, put it together." He grunted. "If anything, my dad has taught me that. To see why things really happen the way they do. Colby's pop runs the jail, he's buds with the DA, and his son is a Benders Hollow god. He knows every detective within a hundred miles of here." He paused. "Colby Morris isn't going to juvie or anywhere else."

I sighed. "God, sometimes life just blows."

"Yeah."

I stared out over the yard, sick of thinking about it. "I need a haircut."

"There's a place in town."

"I want you to do it."

He gave me a suspicious stare. "I don't do haircuts. Especially on girlfriends. Dangerous territory."

"I'll kiss you."

He stood, looking around. "Where are those pesky scissors?"

"Not scissors. Come on." We went inside, to Dad's bathroom, and I searched under the sink, finding what I wanted.

Theo looked. "What?"

I plugged in the clippers. "I said no scissors."

"You want me to shave you? Like bald? Are you turning neo-Nazi on me?"

"No."

"What, then? You want me to shave Velveeta's name in your head to ease the guilt?"

"Shut up. We'll be giving me a traditional punk haircut today."

He smiled, looking at my hair. "Serious? The traditional?"

I nodded. "One Mohawk, please."

He held up a lock of my hair, measuring. "Tall spikes? We could get a good five-inch lift."

"Yeah. I've got some stuff called Concrete. It'll hold it up just fine."

"You'll look like that drummer guy from Blink 182. What's his name, Barker."

"Maybe his sister."

"Is this a spontaneous thing in honor of Velveeta or just a general slap-in-the-face-to-the-establishment-type deal?"

"A general thing. I've done it before." I sat on the toilet, draping a towel over my shoulders. "Make it good. Straight lines. Not too thick on the strip."

"I think you should take your shirt off for this. I don't want to get any hair on it."

"Ha."

"Trade for the kiss?"

Having sex with Theo flashed through my mind, but it was just that. A flash. "Nope. You can settle on your kiss."

"Can I feel your butt during the kiss? Just a little bit?"

I gave him a seductive stare. "Maybe. Get started, slave boy."

"Yes, mistress. At your command."

•   •   •

A half hour and quite a bit of nervous sweat on Theo's part later, I stood in front of the mirror gooping Concrete Water-Resistant Gel into my Mohawk. My black hair covered the bathroom floor, and Theo admired his work. "I think I might have found my true calling. Sex for haircuts."

"Kissing isn't sex." I looked in the mirror. He'd done a great job.

"It could be construed as sex. There are bodily fluids passed."

"Spit doesn't count."

"You make it sound so romantic, Poe."

I turned around, laying my wrists over his shoulders and turning my head. "You like the new do?"

He looked at my hair. "Sexy punker chicks make my blood boil."

The next thing I knew, I was sitting on the bathroom counter, Theo between my legs and his lips on mine. His hands roamed my back and the tingles ran through me like wildfire, and my breathing quickened. His did, too, and his hands went under my shirt, moving up my sides. He flicked his tongue through my teeth, and things definitely went from warm to hot.

"Uh, hello."

Theo was off me like an African jumping spider, and my dad stood in the hall, his hands in his pockets. I straightened, pulling my shirt down and wiping my mouth self-consciously. "Hi, Dad. Uh, sorry."

"Hello, Mr. Holly," Theo cut in, a look of pure fear on his face.

Dad cleared his throat. "Okay." He took a breath. "Well, I see you've got a new hairstyle."

I stepped forward, thankful. When confronted with super-incredibly uncomfortable situations, ignore it. For once, I agreed with my dad. "You like it?"

He studied it, then smiled. "Actually, I think I do. Different."

I looked at the floor. "Really? You're not mad? Mom flipped when I did it before."

He smiled wider. "Honestly, I do like it."

I looked to the floor. "I'll clean this up."

Theo bent down, picking up strands of hair. "Yeah, me too, Mr. Holly. We'll take care of it. Is there anything else you'd like me to do? Wash your car? Paint your house?"

He laughed. "It's okay, Theo. There's a handheld vacuum in the hall closet." He turned, then turned back. "Theo, would you care to stay for dinner?"

"Uh, I can't. My mom is sick."

Dad nodded. "I think it would be nice if you did sometime."

"Yessir."

After Dad left, Theo exhaled. "That was great. Jeez."

"We were just kissing, Theo."

"I was feeling you up. That's not just kissing. Your dad saw me with my hands up your shirt. God."

"Well, it's not like we're twelve."

"Yeah, but . . ."

"You know, for such a rebel-type dude, you sure are a sissy."

He looked at the floor, picking up hair. "It's not that."

I laughed. "Then what is it?"

He wouldn't look up. "You."

"What's that supposed to mean?"

He looked at me, a handful of my hair in his hand. "I like you. That's all. And I don't want to make things bad. I make things bad."

I smiled. He was a romantic. My rebel romantic who spent his time thinking about pop machines and how the world worked. "You won't."

He picked up more hair, chuckling. "If there's one thing Theo Dorr is good at, it's screwing things up. It's my life story."

I knelt beside him, picking up hair. "Fine, then. We'll screw things up together."

• • •

Dad made fajitas and Mexican corn for dinner, and we ate in the den, watching the news in avoidance of what I knew would come. Some things were like the sun coming up in the morning and going down in the evening, and Dad was no exception. He rolled a fajita, taking a bite. "I suppose we should have a talk."

"The birds and the bees?"

"Are you on birth control?"

I took a bite, talking with my mouth full to irritate my anal father. "I've never had sex."

152

"Have you thought about it?"

"Sure. But not until I'm ready."

"You and Theo seem pretty serious."

"You mean because he had his hands up my shirt?"

Dead silence, with the talking head on the news filling in. Dad wiped his mouth. "I'd prefer abstinence, but if you need something, don't hesitate, okay?"

"I know, Dad. My mom is a doctor, remember? I've had it drilled into my head since I started eating solids."

He paused. "I think maybe if Theo is over, you should stay out of your room."

I rolled my eyes. "You'd rather us have sex on the couch?"

He sighed. "That's not what I'm saying. But there have to be some rules in this house. I'm responsible for you, and I've a right to let my opinion be known."

I felt like hugging him. Finally. An opinion. "Gotcha. How about the door stays open?"

"Deal." He sat back and folded his hands over his stomach. "Things seem to be moving so fast. Is it this way with Mom?"

I laughed. "You're used to everything being the same all the time because you're old and infirm. And no, it wasn't this way with Mom."

"Why not?"

I looked at him, wondering what it would have been like to grow up with him. I wondered if I'd be different. "Because she's never around."

He paused, and a good minute or so went by. "Why did you do that to your hair?"

"I wanted something more feminine. You know, stylish."

He laughed. "A statement."

"Let me guess, you think I'm being reactionary."

He smiled, took a moment, then shrugged. "Actually, Poe, I do. But maybe you're right. Maybe sometimes the tree does need to be shaken."

"What's going to happen with Colby?"

"I don't know, but I want you to steer clear of him."

"He's psycho."

"Avoid him, Poe."

"That's your answer to everything, isn't it? Avoid sex, avoid bullies, avoid conflict, avoid injustice, play by the rules. Standard procedure. I think Theo's right."

"What is Theo right about?"

I stared at him. "That it's all the small things we accept that makes this world such a crappy place."

Chapter Nineteen

Fifth hour came the next day with the office administration buzzing our class. Poe Holly was to report to the student office immediately. You'd think nobody in the history of Benders Hollow had ever seen a Mohawk before. Not a single person had said a word to me about it, though, and I'd enjoyed that. Silence was golden sometimes.

I grabbed my things, uneasy with what might be going on, and walked, taking my time. Colby hadn't been in current affairs for third hour, and there'd been no rumor about what was going on other than some sort of investigation. Velveeta wasn't in school, either.

Ms. Appleway smiled when she saw me, her eyes twinkling as she studied my Mohawk. "Glad to see you back, Poe."

"Thanks." I looked toward Vice Principal Avery's office. "In there?"

She shook her head, some of the twinkle leaving her eyes. "No. Your father's office."

"Is this about me, or is it about Colby Morris?"

The twinkle disappeared. She leaned forward, lowering

her voice. "His name is Mr. Dwight Worthy, retired Highway Patrol detective and the district investigator. He's waiting."

I walked past Mr. Avery's office and down the hall, expecting to see my dad sitting with Mr. Worthy. He was nowhere to be found. Mr. Worthy sat at his desk, reading a file. My file, I was sure. I stood at the door. He didn't look up. "Please take a seat, young lady."

I did. He looked up, taking me in without expression. Bald on top, his head was shaved to stubble, the white collar of his dress shirt tight around a thick neck. Age weathered his face, and I figured he was around sixty. His eyes were blue and flat behind silver reading glasses, and his shoulders filled out the chair. He looked exactly like what he was supposed to look like. A cop. He peered at me over the rims of his glasses. "Poe Holly."

I narrowed my eyes. "Dwight Worthy."

He stared with his polished and rock-hard cop eyes, years of practice coming through. "Detective Worthy."

"*Retired* detective Worthy."

The only sign of irritation was a minuscule slump of his big shoulders. His eyes went to my file. "I take it you know why you're here."

"Colby Morris."

"You witnessed the alleged assault?"

"It wasn't alleged."

"Tell me what happened."

I did, and for the next five minutes, he listened without a blink, studying me as I spoke. He sat back when I finished, cocking his fingers under his chin and rubbing. "And you know why this allegedly happened?"

"I told you it's not alleged."

"Please answer the question."

"It happened."

He ignored that statement. "You have an idea why?"

I told him about slapping Anna and Colby thinking Velveeta did it.

"And that's why you went into the lavatory?"

"Yes. I knew something would happen when I saw them drag him in. Why are you acting like you don't believe what happened?"

"I know something happened, Ms. Holly, but I don't know what happened. It's my job to find out."

"Why don't you ask Velveeta or Colby or half the football team? They were there."

"I have. You are the only one who is talking."

"So Velveeta got the shit kicked out of him by a ghost in the boys' bathroom. Mr. Halvorson came in, too. He saw him under the sink."

"Mr. Halvorson wasn't a witness to the act, and the statement your friend Andrew gave doesn't support an assault. He maintains he fell."

It took me a second to remember Vel's real name was Andrew. "This is a bunch of crap. You know what happened."

"I may think I know, but I have no cooperation from the victim."

"Is the DA going to press charges?"

"At this point, no. The victim is refusing to acknowledge any assault occurred, and of course the suspect maintains his innocence."

"So what happens?"

"Unless I can get a statement from Andrew, nothing. The district will record an injury due to slipping and falling, just as he said."

I studied him. "Colby Morris is going to kill him. You know that, don't you?"

"I don't know that, Ms. Holly. I know something happened, and I know there's bad blood between the two, but I can't do anything about it."

"There's not bad blood between the two, there's Colby Morris being a psycho. Velveeta has never done anything to him. Besides that, I'm sitting here telling you Colby Morris was in the bathroom and that he did it."

He shook his head. "That's unsubstantiated without support from Andrew, Ms. Holly."

"My dad told me the DA could press charges without Velveeta if he wanted to."

"Not without proof that the suspect was at least in the same place as the victim." He studied me over his glasses. "Andrew has had quite a traumatic past, hasn't he?"

"What does that have to do with this?"

He ignored me, going on. "Has he talked to you about Colby Morris? Said anything about him at all?"

"What are you getting at?"

"If Colby Morris did in fact beat Andrew, rarely does something this severe happen without some sort of patterned provocation or history. Colby Morris has no previous police record of misconduct, he's an honor roll student, and he's being considered by several colleges for football scholarships. If he did attack Andrew, it seems that there should be some history. Some reason." He eyed me. "Is there a history between you two? Any conflicts?"

I couldn't believe this was happening. "I get it now."

"You get what, Ms. Holly?"

"You're not looking to get Colby, you're looking to whitewash this whole thing."

"I'm investigating all of the possibilities. For the district to make a decision, I have to have the whole story for them. We're dealing with the entire future of a young man, Ms. Holly, and I take that seriously."

I stood. He'd just put the whole thing in perspective. They were dealing with the future of *one* young man, and it wasn't Velveeta. "You're full of crap, Mr. Worthy."

He grimaced. "We're not done, Ms. Holly. Sit down."

"Why? So you can figure out why I would make up a story about Colby Morris?" I crossed my arms and rolled my eyes. "Let me guess. You think I beat Velveeta up, blamed it on Colby Morris, and Velveeta is protecting me because he's madly in love with the woman who tried to kill him in the boys' bathroom? That would be convenient if it was a TV show. The only reason you're here is to figure out how the district can get out of this without losing a lawsuit." I shook my head. "We're done." Then I walked out.

On the way past Ms. Appleway, I took my ID badge from around my neck and flung it on the counter. "This place sucks." Halfway down the hall, I stopped. Class was in, and the place looked like a ghost town. I stood at the doors to the courtyard staring across the emptiness, then looked up, thinking about what Detective Doorknob said about pressing charges. I turned around and walked back to the office. "Ms. Appleway?"

She looked up. My badge still lay on the counter. "Yes?"

I leaned over the counter. "Remember when Theo and I switched ID cards?"

She nodded.

"How specific are they?"

"What do you mean?"

I thought. "I mean, if you pulled my name up on the computer, could you tell I was here right now?"

"Not exactly. I could tell what time you came in the building, what rooms you entered and exited, and what time you left the building, which would give me a good idea. Unless of course you went through a window. Then it would only tell me when you came in, but it would pick up what building or room you went in next."

"So the sensors don't keep total track of you?"

"No. Just the entry time and exit time."

"Does it keep a record of it?"

"Yes, but only for three days. The system only keeps truancies on file for longer. Otherwise it would overload."

"Could you do me a favor?"

"What?"

"Look up Colby Morris for me? Tuesday between nine-thirty and ten-thirty?"

She thought for a moment. "I've heard the story, Poe."

"Then you know what I want. He was in there, Ms. Appleway. You know he did it."

Her fingers flew over the keyboard, punching in Colby's name. A few seconds later, she turned the computer screen toward me. "See that list? That's the list of all the sensors he tripped from nine-thirty to ten-thirty." She studied it, then pointed. "Okay. There it is. He left second-period room 132, the metal shop, three minutes early. Twenty seconds later

160

he left the shop building, and thirty seconds after that he entered the main building. Sensor number 2234 was tripped at nine fifty-two. It was tripped again at nine fifty-nine."

I swallowed. "What sensor is that?"

She smiled. "The boys' bathroom." Her hands flew over the keyboard again, a sly look on her face, and a moment later she reached under the counter and pulled out a sheet of paper. "Here it is."

I took it, smiling as I folded it in my pocket. "That puts him there."

Her smile widened. "It would seem so."

"Will you get in trouble for this?"

"I know of no policy disallowing it." She shrugged. "I'm sure they'll make one up after this, but that's another day, now isn't it?"

"Thanks."

She picked up my ID card. "You'll need this."

I took it, searching her face. She was different. Different from anybody in this school. "Why do you work here?"

She looked at me, then smiled, brushing it off. "I was a teacher for twenty-two years."

"But you don't like this school, do you?"

She looked away, her old lady glasses catching the glint of the fluorescent lights above. "Sometimes a school loses sight of why it exists."

I frowned. "How?"

She smiled, patting the computer monitor like a mangy pet robot dog. "Us old hacks call the school system The Beast for a reason, Poe, and even though it serves a high purpose, sometimes common sense and logic are lost in the politics."

"You sound like Theo."

She chuckled. "I spent almost three decades coming to work for something I believe in. Still do. The pendulum swings, though, and sometimes"—she eyed me—"somebody needs to make it swing the other way. Now off with you," she said, shooing me away.

Chapter Twenty

The only problem with living in a small town is that the avoidance factor is impossible unless you dig a hole and bury yourself. Everybody knows everybody, everybody knows who knows everybody, and you can't avoid anybody. It was like walking around in a fishbowl, and any kind of privacy was like politics and honesty. Impossible.

Anna Conrad waited at my locker after sixth period, her lip still swollen. I opened my locker. "How's your face?"

She set her jaw. "We need to talk."

I stepped closer. The urge to take a handful of that beautiful golden hair and pull it out consumed every fiber of my being. I could almost feel the blond filaments clenched in my fist.

She looked around, maybe hoping to find a friend, or an armor-plated Humvee, in the students swarming around us. "I didn't know Colby would do that."

I stared at her for a moment, and the anger slipped away almost as fast as it had come. I felt like I was staring at a first grader who'd accidentally set off a nuclear bomb and had no idea what was going on. "You're a sad little skank, you know that? Anna Conrad the pretty girl who didn't know. Boo hoo." I grimaced. "Go make yourself feel better somewhere else."

She cleared her throat, then took a breath. Tears welled in her eyes. "Is he all right?"

I stared at her. "No, he's not. But maybe you should drop on by with some cookies to make everything all better, huh?" I sneered. "Flip your skirt and show some ass and everything will be just fine, because we all know Anna Conrad can't do anything wrong."

She furrowed her brow. "What does that mean?"

"It means you suck."

She looked me up and down, her face twisting in anger before she took a breath. "I'm trying to apologize."

"Is that what it says in the Anna Conrad handbook of how to do things right?"

She looked down and away. "Shut up. It's not that way."

I laughed. "Yes, it is, Anna."

She hesitated, then drew herself up. "I was trying to apologize to you in the hall when you slapped me. About choir. I don't think it's right, but my parents pushed it. And I do feel horrible about the letter. I didn't think they were going to do that, and if I'd known, I wouldn't have written it. They said it was all in fun. Just a prank. Colby has had it out for Velveeta since he got here, but I never thought he'd take it this far."

"Well, he did, didn't he?"

Her eyes flashed. "Yes, he did. But I didn't. And you can't blame me for that."

I shut my locker. "You're a rotten person, Anna, and the sick part is that you're too stupid to see it."

"It's not my fault."

I turned. "Don't worry, Anna, everybody knows you're an angel. Little Anna who didn't know is always a perfect little angel."

Her voice rose above the chatter of the few remaining students in the hall. "You're a bitch, you know that? You're the one who started this, and you know it, so don't put it on me."

I walked back up to her, ready to knock her teeth out. "What do you want, Anna? You want me to say it's all right? You want me to say you're not a rotten person?" I glared. "It's not going to happen. I don't like you and I never will."

Her hand came out of nowhere, and the slap echoed down the hall. Heads turned, and as my cheek burned, I stared. Her mouth was a slit, her own cheeks flush and red. "I told you I DID NOT KNOW it was going to happen. Any of it. And I don't want you to like me or need you to like me. I just wanted to try and make things as right as I could, because I know I was wrong."

She was ready, and I knew it would be a heck of a fight. It surprised me. Anna Conrad had a backbone. I touched my cheek. "Wow."

She sniffed, then took a deep breath. "You're the one with the problems, you know that? Ever since you came here, you act like everybody is below you." She stared. "You're the stuck-up bitch, Poe, not me."

Chapter Twenty-one

"His car was totally smashed. We're talking baseball bat city. All the windows, everything."

Sunday afternoon waned away with the boredom only Benders Hollow could offer, and up to now I'd been wandering aimlessly around the house like an old woman with dementia. Until Theo knocked on the door.

Now this. Theo and I sat on the front porch as a bruised and stitched Velveeta dug dandelions from his yard. I watched as he spit a wad of tobacco between his knees, bending back down to the never-ending supply of yellow-headed weeds infesting the lawn. He'd told me his aunt didn't believe in the chemical assassination of weeds on account of harming the environment. "You think he did it?"

Theo laughed. "Who else would trash Colby's car?" He looked toward Velveeta. "The guy's got a death wish, Poe."

"And I suppose Colby thinks he did it."

"Oh yeah. Football man is on the warpath. Even with the little 'investigation' going on. He told Mark Garvey he was going to bust Velveeta's arms, and I believe it."

"Great."

Theo shrugged. "Monday will be interesting."

I'd told Theo about Detective Worthy, and he'd met my story with the typical Theo sarcasm I loved. I shifted from one butt cheek to the other. "So he gets away scot-free and Velveeta's going to die. Great."

"Life in rural America isn't what it seems."

"We've got to do something."

"I've been thinking about that, too."

"You have?"

He fiddled with his shoelace. "Yeah. If we sneak up and hit him on the head hard enough, most likely from behind and with something large and heavy, we can drag his body out to a remote vineyard, chop him up into little pieces, and feed him to the squirrels."

I rolled my eyes. "Brilliant."

He shook his head. "Not really. I couldn't remember if squirrels were carnivores or not, but I think they might be if they're hungry enough." He leaned back. "I'm also squeamish about cutting people into small chunks, so that poses a problem unless you do that part."

I watched as my dad pulled into the driveway. "I'm not the murdering type."

"Me neither, but I could be an accomplice or something. Like a *Pulp Fiction* type of gig. You saw it, right?"

"Yeah."

"Travolta rocks, but Samuel Jackson made it what it was. Legendary shit."

Dad walked up the path. He nodded, a sack of books in one hand. "Hi, guys."

"Hi."

He gazed over at Velveeta, then focused on us. "What are you two up to?"

"Nothing."

He smiled, nodding to the books in the sack. "Hey, we're going to be putting on an anti-harassment seminar at the school tomorrow to promote awareness. Would you two like to attend?"

Being a good puppy in front of my dad, Theo agreed enthusiastically. I rolled my eyes. "Sure."

"You don't like that idea, Poe?"

"Isn't that like inviting criminals to drop on by the jail and turn themselves in?"

He shrugged. "Perhaps, but we've got to start somewhere." He opened the screen door. "You'll get out of sixth period."

I smiled. "I'm there."

After Dad went in, I smacked Theo on the side of the head. "Loser."

"Hey, what? I'm always into social awareness programs. Anything to make the cogs in the collective machinery run smoothly."

"Yeah, sure."

He laughed. "Well, he's right in an oddball kind of way."

"It's bullshit. So a bunch of victims and bleeding hearts get together and talk about how bad their lives are, have a good cry, then my dad and Halvorson get up and tell them how to be better punching bags. I've seen it happen before, and this place is no different."

He shrugged. "Well, if you're going to be a punching bag, be the best one you can be. That's what my dad always says."

"It's just stupid."

"Of course it's stupid, but at least he's trying. It's not like he can unleash a herd of meat-eating squirrels in the halls and watch the carnage begin."

I laughed. "Yeah, but it's lip service."

"We'll see. Sixth period tomorrow. Be there or be square."

Chapter Twenty-two

Monday burned by like a slow day in hell.

The rumor mill was buzzing on high frequency, though, and by second period it was like a riptide sucking everybody under with it. Colby's pissed. Velveeta's dead. Did you hear? Oh my God, the shit is going to hit the fan. I was so sick of it by current affairs third period I almost left. Velveeta was nowhere to be found.

I knew Halvorson knew about the car thing. You'd have to be dead not to know what was going on, and by the looks he gave Colby, I was right. I couldn't tell if he was expecting World War III to erupt or was praying to the god of public education for a break in the action.

I figured Velveeta was lying low because he knew Colby would be after him, but I wasn't sure. I wasn't even sure Velveeta bashed his car. I hoped he hadn't, but I knew it didn't make a difference anyway. Colby Morris and Velveeta were going to meet in the end in a bad way, and nothing could stop it.

Mr. Halvorson chose to give an hour-long monologue concerning the intricacies of the Patriot Act, which, while protecting us, has given the Homeland Security Department carte blanche to rip the Constitution to shreds. He thought differently, though, basically explaining that the security of our free nation was more important than focusing on trivial things like freedom.

Next came PE, and with so much on my mind, I'd given up on the uniform issue. I'd be a peon and wear my stupid shirt. When I got to the locker room, most of the class had already suited up and were in the gym, and as I took my uniform from the shelf in the locker, I sighed, stared at it, thought about what I should do, then put it away.

I walked into the gym wearing the shirt I'd worn to school, and Coach Policheck stood in front of the girls, hands on her hips. She glanced over at me, her jaw set in what my mom called angry stone. She raised her voice. "Are you happy now, Ms. Holly?" I stopped, looking at the line of girls. At least half of them, including Anna Conrad, wore their street shirts. No uniforms. I didn't reply but stepped past her and took my place in line. Coach Policheck shot me a look. "Well, now that everybody is here, we may begin. Those students who chose not to wear a uniform to class will immediately excuse themselves to the locker room to change. If not, punishment will follow. Mutiny is not allowable at this school."

I kept my smile inside. If mutiny was allowed, it wouldn't be called a mutiny. Vice Principal Avery would need a bigger office, it seemed. Coach Policheck stood waiting, even tapping her toe, and nobody stepped out. Coach took a deep breath in through her nose, then exhaled, her voice echoing across the gym. "This ENTIRE class will be given detention for three days if those who are not wearing their uniforms don't excuse themselves to the locker room."

Nobody moved. The boys at the other end stared, smiling, laughing, and shaking their heads. Coach Policheck grunted, taking up her clipboard and pen while she walked down the line, checking names. Once finished, she faced us again. "I will be speaking to Vice Principal Avery about suspensions for each of you not wearing your uniform." She pointed to the bleachers beyond the volleyball nets. "You may take a seat until such a time that you wear your uniforms. Excused!"

Half the class, over twenty-five girls, sat on the bleachers watching the other half play volleyball. I sat on the top row, my back against the wall. Anna Conrad hopped up next to me, silent.

I looked across the gym, knowing the answer before I asked it. "You did this, didn't you?"

Silence.

"Why?"

She shrugged. "I quit choir today."

"Why?" I said, holding back my surprise.

"My own reasons."

"You think this changes anything?"

She stared across the gym. "I don't care if it changes anything." We sat for a few moments, all the while Coach Policheck throwing us disgusted glances. "So this is what it feels like," she continued.

"What?"

"Not doing what you're told to do."

I sat back, the brick wall cool. "You always do what you're told to do, don't you?"

"Yes."

"So now you want to be a rebel."

"I've spent my whole life doing everything I'm supposed to do. Being an angel."

I smirked. "Well, I still don't like you."

"I don't like you, either. And the hair is stupid."

I laughed, looking at her low-cut tee with her cleavage hanging out. "Better than letting my boobs hang out so people will pay attention to me."

"Same thing, isn't it?"

I thought about it. Damn, she was making it hard to hate her. "I guess."

"You have no idea how much trouble I'm going to be in."

I smiled. "My mom is a doctor. Rebellion isn't well liked around our place."

"Let me guess. Gone all the time and on your case when she's around."

I nodded. "Same with you?"

She shook her head. "No. They're always around. It never ends. My mom thinks she's me."

A wave of guilty pleasure ran through me, but the guilt, something I wasn't too familiar with, seeped a bit deeper than I liked. "Why'd you quit choir?"

She watched as a ball sailed into the bleachers, bouncing toward us before a girl caught it and threw it back to the court. "It's unfair what they did to you. You're better than I am." She paused. "My parents went off the wall about it, you know."

I smirked. "So why did you quit, though?"

She shrugged. "I hate singing."

I sighed, catching a fractious glimpse of the side of her life I didn't want to know about. The reasons why. It sucked, because I understood what she was talking about. Having a mother who wanted you to be something other than you were sucked, and it could make you hate the things you really loved. "You're awesome, though."

"Oh well."

Moments passed, and I didn't know what to say. I didn't know what it meant as far as choir went. Would I have the spot? Was it too late? The guilt came back, though, shadowing everything. "You shouldn't have quit."

She wouldn't meet my eyes, and she lowered her voice enough that it was hard to hear her over the screech of tennis shoes and echoed shouts on the courts below. "I've wanted to quit for a long time."

I shook my head. "You're full of crap for letting them ruin it for you."

"You don't know anything."

"Yeah, I do."

"No, you don't. You don't know me, and you don't know my mom."

I rolled my eyes. "Fine. I don't know you, and honestly, I hope I never meet your mom."

"Yeah." She looked across the gym, and her voice softened. "I heard you were in a band."

"Yeah."

"Fun?"

I smiled, missing the guys. "The best. We're good." I paused. "Well, we were until I screwed things up and came here."

She looked away. "It sounds fun."

Awkward silence. I pictured her singing in a band like the Go-Go's or Bananarama. "You should try it."

She tightened her ponytail, ignoring the comment. "Are you going to the harassment awareness seminar today?"

"Yes. Theo and I are going."

She stood. "See you there, then."

• • •

The seminar was in the library, and when Theo and I arrived, I noticed a piece of paper hastily scribbled with "LOSERS—→" taped to the wall. Theo smiled. "Well, I guess we're home."

"Ha ha," I said, then saw Anna in the room, looking like a fish out of water. My guess was that most of her friends wouldn't be coming primarily because the reason this was being held was due to most of her friends. We went in and sat next to her. "Where's your friends?" I said.

She looked around, like somebody she knew would actually be here. "I told them to come."

Theo scratched his ear, maybe wondering if she was seriously being serious. "Whoever steps in here is instantly branded a social leper muddling through the waste of a perfect society, Anna. Pull your head out of your ass, huh? They're not coming."

I sighed. Theo the drama queen. "God, Theo, you should be an actor."

He laughed. "I would be Romeo and you would be Juliet." He looked at Anna. "Going to the Night of Stars football fund-raiser picnic tomorrow, Anna?"

She looked down. "I'm a cheerleader, Theo. It's required."

He smiled, nudging me. "It's a gala festival full of fun and games for the entire family. Wanna go, Poe?"

"Fat chance," I said. Theo scrunched up his face like a guilt-ridden kid with an admission. I stared at him in disbelief. "Don't even tell me . . ."

He shrugged. "My dad is a huge contributor. He calls my attendance familial duty."

I rolled my eyes. "You have no backbone."

"Will you go with me? Pleeeeezzzz? You can protect me from the big bad guys."

"No."

He tilted his head, pouting. "I'd do it for you. Besides, the food is really good. Almost like a buffet but without people stuffing pork ribs in their pockets for later. And you get to laugh at two-hundred-and-fifty-pound linebackers tossing eggs."

"Sounds like an all-American evening."

"It'll be fun. I promise."

I twirled a finger. "Woo hoo. I'm there."

Theo smiled. "Really?"

"Sure." I pecked him on the cheek. "You came to this, I guess I owe payback."

Just like every other aspect of high school in the United States, I could tell who was who as students filtered into the room. The uglies, the fatties, the dorks, the dweebs, the shorties, the socially inept, and the just plain weird mixed with the regulars who didn't know a thing about being a reject but who were there because they had some sort of humanitarian cause. Everybody wore their badge of rank by the expressions on their faces: the meek, desperate, homely, fearful, disaffected, glum, pained, and starved looks of people that just plain didn't fit in. Even with each other.

I figured I fit right in, but I had little pity for them. They reminded me of sheep grazing in a DDT-coated pasture, not realizing the thing that was feeding them was the thing that was killing them. I felt like laughing at the irony of it all, then giving them the finger and leaving. They accepted their places and this charade, just like Theo said. Cogs in a wheel. For there to be the strong, there had to be the weak, and I didn't know if I hated them or the world more because of it. Maybe Anna had been right, I thought. Maybe I was the elitist one.

Mr. Halvorson took front and center, smiling and rubbing his hands together like he was getting ready to give a sermon to the ugly class. Dad sat in a chair with his legs crossed like a chick, his hands folded over his knee, and I rolled my eyes. My attitude definitely wasn't going to be a bonus today.

"Thank you for coming," Mr. Halvorson began. "We at Benders High are devoted to maintaining a standard of equality and fairness for every student setting foot inside our buildings, and that is why we're here. To discuss how we can make an outstanding school even more outstanding . . ."

Theo raised his hand.

Caution flashed in Mr. Halvorson's eyes, but in the spirit of gooshy-gooshy feel-good meetings, he acquiesced. "Yes, Mr. Dorr?"

"I just wanted to say that as a total loser, I feel lucky to go to such an outstanding school. It makes me feel less loser-like."

Mr. Halvorson took a breath. "May I finish my introduction before we begin speaking of our feelings?" He waited a moment, then nodded after Theo shut up. "Both Mr. Holly and myself realize just how difficult being a teenager can be these days, but the simple fact of the matter is that we aren't teenagers. We're adults. And this seminar was designed for you, as teenagers going through a difficult period, to let us know. To tell us your feelings and let us help you deal with them in the ways we, as adults, know how. How to deal with isolation, estrangement, depression, and inequity, and, in essence, how to be a better you. A more happy you."

If there was a cheese meter on the wall, it would have exploded, and as he finished, a moment of awkward silence followed before a few people clapped. Mr. Halvorson slapped his hands together like a Little League coach telling his team to take the field, and I expected him to start handing down high fives, but he didn't. He cleared his throat. "Well, down to business, then." He paused. "How many of you have felt as though you don't quite fit in? Maybe felt as though who you are isn't really who you wish you were?"

A few hands went up, heads turned in the crowd, checking out the possibility of social embarrassment taking place at the social embarrassment seminar, then more hands went up. Soon most had their hands up. Theo held his up high, waggling his wrist like a little kid. I sighed when he elbowed me, then put my hand up. Anna didn't.

Mr. Halvorson nodded. "Good."

I looked around, confused. What was good about a room full of people holding their hands up claiming to be miserable and wishing they were somebody else? I looked at my dad, who had his own hand up to make us feel like we were all in the same sinking ship, and I pinned my lips shut. He should have asked how many people would scrape their skins off with a dull knife to be left alone for five

178

minutes, but that wasn't about to happen. We'd stick to the feel-sorry stuff.

As usual, a few people kept their hands up until Mr. Halvorson told them gently to put them down, then he went on. "I would like to tell each and every one of you that the feelings you have are feelings everybody has at one time or another and that they're normal." He gazed over us. "What I'm saying is that everybody is the same. We all have the same feelings, and we're all human. The difference is"—he paced—"the difference is how we deal with those feelings and what tools we have to work with them. That's what this seminar is about."

The reasons were adding up, but the real reason wasn't anywhere to be found. The reason we were here wasn't because we were all the same; we were here because a kid almost got the life stomped out of him in the boys' bathroom and they had to do damage control for it.

Mr. Halvorson motioned to my dad, then took a seat as Dad stood. His eyes flickered to me, then roamed the room. "What I would like to do is begin with stories. Real stories. Stories that show us what we have in common and stories that show us the truth about the world we live in. I'd like to know where you are coming from, and the best way to know is to hear your stories." He paced. "All of you have experienced harassment of some sort. I have, too. Bullying, teasing, verbal abuse, physical abuse, humiliation, and embarrassment—we've all had some of it, and we can take comfort that we're not alone. But we can also be proactive in stopping it. We can make ourselves strong." He stepped forward. "Would anyone like to begin?"

Big, noisy silence. I wasn't about to gush my guts out

179

about what a victim I was, because I wasn't, and my dad had another thing coming if he thought I would bail him out by starting. Then a fat girl raised her hand. Dad nodded, motioned for her to stand, and she began. Fatso, fat ass, fat bitch, tub of lard—she started with what people called her. Her dad called her tubby, she wouldn't eat in public because guys made oinking noises, she'd never had a boyfriend and never would, and she hated herself and perspired too much. By the time she was done, tears rolled down her cheeks, and she sat, burying her face in her hands and sobbing. Let the healing begin.

The next half hour came with one story after another about the injustices of being who you were, and I realized halfway into it that soaking in the brine of your misery became easy when other people were around doing the same thing. I found myself almost thinking this was serving another purpose than damage control over the Velveeta thing, and it made me uncomfortable. It was like a mass celebration of victimhood, with the coup de grace being the Kool-Aid passed around at the end. There was even a kid sitting up front who looked a little bit like Jim Jones.

It went on. The skinny dork with acne and secondhand clothes who didn't have any friends, probably the most innocuous one of them all, had half the room crying by the time he finished talking about being constantly berated and teased, especially by the wrestling team. He'd tried out last year at the urging of his parents to "fit in" and didn't make the cut, inviting the team's wrath and ridicule. He spoke in a lifeless monotone, spelling out his world like he was reading it from a textbook, and I realized he was most likely the loneliest human being that ever lived.

There were others. The short guy named Kevin who dreaded coming to school because he was stuffed in garbage cans every week. The straight guy who acted gay and was tormented constantly about being a fag. The loud-mouthed girl who couldn't seem to figure out why other girls hated her. The kid they called "Teenie" who got the nickname from the boys' locker room. It was like a celebration of sick diversity, and it made me want to puke.

After everybody who had something to say was emotionally spent, Mr. Halvorson stood, a grave and compassionate look on his face. He paced, building on the moment before he began. "We know what happens in this world. We know sometimes it's unfair and mean and painful, but what we have to do is look inside ourselves and see the true us. The true person inside. The person we really are and the person who wants to shake off the chains of our differences and be at one with ourselves and the people around us. Do you agree?"

A few nods before he pointed to the ceiling, shaking his finger. "The key to that is realizing that we are all indeed the same. The boy who calls you a name or the girl who ignores you has feelings, too. Feelings of pain and anger and sadness that make them do what they do, and feelings that cause them to hurt other people. We need to understand that and realize that we're not different." He stopped, looking over the room with an expectant air. "So now I ask you, what can we do when faced with adversity? Should we separate ourselves through harsh words and bad feelings and feelings of isolation, or should we have the courage and compassion it takes to understand why this is happening? To shape our thinking differently?"

181

He pointed to the kid with acne. "Karl, how do you feel when you are ridiculed? Like running to your room? Disappearing? Isolating yourself from the world because you don't want to deal with it?"

"No."

He pursed his lips. "Then why do you go to your room?"

Karl's dead flat voice hushed the room. "Because nobody is there."

Mr. Halvorson nodded. "You go to your room because nobody is there. Isn't that running away from the problem?"

"Maybe."

"Do you wish it was different? That you didn't feel as though you had to run?"

"Yes."

Mr. Halvorson nodded, smiling. "What do you wish you could do?"

"Kill them."

Mr. Halvorson took a deep breath, then went on. "Though perhaps understandable at times, don't you think that's a bit extreme?"

"No."

Mr. Halvorson cleared his throat, maybe thinking he had come here to talk about the dangers of prancing through the daisies. "Do you think there's something else you could do that might be better? Perhaps telling a teacher or parent? Perhaps talking to your counselor?"

His eyes, as flat as his voice, bored into Mr. Halvorson. "I've been in private counseling for two years. I've also talked to Mr. Holly. So have my parents."

He nodded. "Very good, because that's why we have

182

things like that. To help you." Mr. Halvorson's body visibly flooded with relief at not having to deal with this kid. He addressed the group. "Does anybody have an idea of what we can do to make things better for Karl? Maybe what he can do?"

I stared at Mr. Halvorson for a moment, considering, then raised my hand. "Why aren't we talking about why you allow them to do it?"

Mr. Halvorson's brow furrowed. "Allow them?"

"Yeah. What you're saying is that we have to deal with the jerks and understand them and all that bullshit, but the jerks don't have to do anything."

Mr. Halvorson blinked. "We can keep this seminar civil, Ms. Holly. Your language . . ."

I rolled my eyes. "You just blew off a guy who told you that he wishes he could kill people, and you want to talk about my language?" I tapped my finger on my chin. "I get it. We can say whatever we want, but only if it looks pretty?"

He glowered. "We're here to solve problems, Poe, and if you choose not to, you may leave. You are off topic."

"I'm off *your* topic, Mr. Halvorson."

"I'm trying to solve problems in a manner that will allow you to help yourselves."

I shook my head. "Solve what problems? Yours or ours?" I pointed to Karl. "He just told you *he wanted to kill people*, and you want to ask for suggestions about how to change his thinking? I don't think Karl has to change anything, Mr. Halvorson. I think you do."

My dad stood, relieving a flustered Mr. Halvorson. Theo chuckled, then patted my knee. Dad crossed his arms. "So

183

you believe it is entirely up to other people to solve your problems, Poe?"

I shook my head. This was the culmination of all the conversations we'd had. Everything rolled up in one big, slimy ball. "That's not the point, because this isn't 'life.' This is school, we're trapped here, and you control it. You make the rules."

"What's the point you're trying to make, then?"

"The point is that all of a sudden, *you have a problem,* and that's why we're here. Not because *we* have a problem." I shook my head. "When *Benders High School* has a problem, Mr. Halvorson gets up and tells us that we have to solve it for them, then gives us a bunch of bullshit about how it's normal to have these feelings and that we have to understand how the ass wipes who make life miserable feel." I pointed to Karl again. "I don't think a kid wanting to murder half the school is normal, and I don't think he got to feeling that way all by himself." I looked at Karl. "Karl, you're not normal. You're fucked in the head, but you know that, don't you?"

Dad interrupted. "Poe, that's enough."

"No." I kept my eyes on Karl. I could almost read his mind. "Who would you kill first, Karl? Come on. Tell us."

He hesitated in the silence of the room. Then he looked at my dad. "You."

Corpses made more noise than the people in the room. Nobody breathed. I nodded. "Why?"

"Because he's supposed to make them quit, but he won't."

Dad shook his head. "That's not true, Karl. I've tried. We have done—"

My voice rose above his. "Have done what? Why don't

184

you tell us what's being done instead of this stupid seminar? An anti-harassment seminar for the wrestling team? Detention? Suspension? Probation? Conflict resolution classes? A change in school policy? Maybe a teacher or two who doesn't ignore it when it happens? You make the rules, right?" I thought about Mr. Halvorson's little speech on the first day of school about "fitting in." "Tell us, because the only reason we're in this room is because Benders High School sees a liability threat with the name Velveeta written all over it and you need to control it. There, I said it. The real reason you even give a fuck. So what happens? Colby Morris and all the superstar guys in the bathroom who watched Velveeta get stomped are business as usual, but we're here listening to a crock of crap from a guy who thinks the world's troubles would be solved if everybody was exactly the same."

Dad shook his head. "That's a separate issue."

Hypocritical statement of the year. I gestured around us. "Then why are we here? The only reason you put this seminar on was because of what 'didn't' happen to Velveeta, so why doesn't the school do something about the guys that 'didn't' do it?" I slumped in my chair. "Tell us, huh?" I jabbed a finger at my dad and Mr. Halvorson. "The only reason they beat the shit out of him is because *they knew they could,* and *this school* gave them the power to do it!" I waved my arms around the room. "God! This seminar even proves it!"

Dad's face tightened. "We're planning to do things, but the first thing we can do is help kids deal with it." He nodded. "Something has to come first, doesn't it?"

"So you think the first thing to do with Velveeta is talk

to him about how to accept why it happened and change his thinking so it won't happen again? If you're not going to be honest about it, you could at least say, 'Hey, losers, you're pretty much on your own, so you'd better fight back or get used to being social punching bags.'"

He sighed. "This is a no-violence zone, Poe, and you know we can't condone any action like that. Or your language."

I laughed, thinking of everything from choir to PE to Colby Morris and how every time my dad didn't want to be honest, he fell back on the bullshit. "Okay, fine. Let me get this straight. After you don't do anything to stop violence in the first place, you tell us that we can't fight back because there's no tolerance for violence." I stared at him. "Aren't you basically telling us that there's no escape from it? God, Dad! What do you expect?"

"Poe . . ."

"NO! I'm right!" I turned to the classroom. "Who here has fought back?"

The short kid who liked getting stuffed into garbage cans raised his hand.

"What happened?"

"I got suspended for fighting."

I turned back to Dad. "So what you're telling him is that he's just as bad as the jerk who harasses him?"

He looked at the gathering of students, all of whom were silent as church mice. "There's a difference between solving a problem and escalating a problem, and that's why we have safeguards to protect you so that it doesn't happen."

I stood. "Safeguards? Like at Columbine?" I said, knowing I'd thrown a bomb into the room. Columbine was better seen as an aberration, something that could happen *there,* not *here.*

"We're not talking about that circumstance, but that's exactly what we're trying to avoid."

"Avoid?" I crossed my arms, growling. "Has it ever occurred to anybody that when you tell the wrong kid they can't fight back, they'll eventually snap? That once Karl has jumped through all of your useless hoops, he might just come to school locked and loaded?"

The lines around Dad's eyes said his patience wore thin. "Again, that's what we're trying to avoid."

I looked over the gathering. "How many people in here have fantasized about killing the people that mess with them?" A few seconds passed, then hands went up. At least ten. I gazed at Halvorson. "Great job! Why don't you just light the fuse and watch it blow, because that's what will happen."

Mr. Halvorson stood. "I don't think we should be talking about killing. This seminar isn't about that, and it's dangerous ground."

I laughed. "Then what the fuck is this seminar about? Random acts of giggling? We shouldn't even be here!" I pointed outside. "They should. Colby Morris and every guy who was in the bathroom should be sitting here getting a ration of shit from you, but they aren't, are they? They're getting ready for their little festival fund-raiser tomorrow, right? The Night of Stars?"

Mr. Halvorson sighed. "We're here to talk about our problems and how we can solve them, Poe, not about accusations and bitterness. And furthermore"—his eyes flicked to my dad, then settled back on me—"I'm asking you to leave this seminar immediately. There is no need for you here, or your vulgarity. Please excuse yourself." With that, he raised his arm and pointed to the door.

I locked eyes with him then, and took a breath. "You just saw ten people raise their hands saying they've thought about MURDER, and what I'm saying is that maybe they wouldn't feel that way if you actually believed in what you preach." I shook my head. "I watched a kid almost get killed in your school because the guy that did it knows you won't do anything. Good job. You suck," I said. Then I left.

Chapter Twenty-three

I left Theo and Anna in the dust, stomping my way home with one thing on my mind. Velveeta. Since Theo told me about Colby's car being bashed, I'd had a sinking feeling about where things were headed, and the seminar only made me rage more. I didn't think things were going to get better before they got worse, and it would be bad. Real bad. And Benders High School wasn't interested in doing a thing about it.

I knocked on Velveeta's door, but nobody answered, so I sat on the porch for ten minutes, knocked again, peeked in his bedroom window on the other side of the house, sat for another half hour, then went inside and sat in front of the window, watching the pictures in my head. I had to do something. Velveeta hadn't been in school, I hadn't seen him, and that meant bad things.

My cell phone minutes had expired three days before I arrived in Benders Hollow, and I was still going through cell withdrawals. I picked up the cordless, dug in my purse for Theo's cell number, and dialed. "Hi. Sorry I ditched you."

He laughed. "Didn't miss much. Just Mr. Halvorson

elaborating on how sinful violence is and that it's never the answer to anything. Unless you're a government, of course. Then you can drop bombs on people's heads all you want."

"Whatever."

"You were right, though. Maybe a bit extreme, but right."

I laughed. "Since when does right matter?"

"When it suits the Man." He paused. "Are we still on for tomorrow's festivities? Always wanted to have my leg tied to yours as we race across a park."

"No."

"Come on, Poe. It's not the end of the world. The school has to do stuff that way."

"I'm not going."

"You said you would."

I thought about it. "Fine. What time?"

"Six-thirty. The football guys need time to rinse the blood off after practice."

That answered the question I called him for, and I was glad I didn't have to ask it. "Cool. See ya tomorrow."

"Bye."

I walked out the door and headed back to the school, checking the church clock on the way. Five-fifteen. I reached the school courtyard and walked through the deserted place, soaking in the silence of the usually crowded area. Almost peaceful if you forgot what it was. I wondered if it could be a good place, then put it out of my mind.

Past the courtyard and between the choir building and gym, I walked around the corner and saw the football team breaking from the field and jogging toward me, their white helmets bobbing up and down against shoulder pads as they headed for the gym doors. The coach jogged behind them, and I stepped aside as the first player clattered past. I heard several Mohawk comments as I searched through the face masks for Colby, and when I saw him, I stepped out, making eye contact. He smiled past the bars of his helmet as he neared, and he veered my way when I called his name, slowing a bit.

As he passed, he leaned his shoulder and did a quick step, catching me hard on my side. Surprised, I lost my balance and fell, sprawling like an idiot as the last players streamed by. I'd landed square on my wrist, and as I sat there rubbing it, the coach stopped and smiled, offering his hand with a chuckle. "Gotta watch out there, girl. Sometimes the boys don't know how much space they take up." I stared at his hand, then slapped it away. He frowned. "Hey, now, there's no need for that. I was offering you a hand."

I stood, brushing myself off. "Go to hell. I need to talk to Colby."

He smiled. "Well, you're welcome to go into the locker room, but I'd advise against it. Might see something you don't want to."

"When I want your advice on how to be a macho jerk, I'll ask." Then I shoved past him and entered the gym. The coach followed, raising his voice for me to stop, but I ignored him and went through the locker room doors.

Deep-voiced laughs and voices clapped against the concrete walls, and the mist of the showers smelled like sweat and fungus as I walked down the far wall, searching down the rows of lockers. Guys stopped what they were doing, some throwing towels over themselves and some not as I neared the showers. Catcalls followed me, and I realized I might have made a mistake.

By the time I found him, most of the team had followed me back to the showers. Colby stood at the tiled entrance to the steamy section, a towel wrapped around his waist and another smart-ass grin on his face. I breathed. "I slapped Anna."

He smiled. "Yeah. I guess you did."

"You almost killed him, Colby."

He laughed, then glanced at the coach, who was walking down the aisle. "I don't know what you're talking about."

I smiled, taking a sheet of paper from my back pocket. The one from Ms. Appleway. I raised my voice as I held the paper over my head, waving it around. "You did it, and this is a record of every single one of you who was in there when it happened." I glanced around and was happy to see some very uncomfortable looks on faces.

Colby snatched the paper from me, crumpling it up and throwing it on the wet floor. "You can't touch me, bitch."

I nodded. "Don't worry, I've got a copy." I walked away, then turned around again. "And Colby?"

He stared at me from down the aisle.

"I *can* touch you," I said. Then I walked out.

Chapter Twenty-four

He didn't say anything. Not a word. Just sat in a front porch chair staring out at the neighborhood in the late-afternoon sunlight. One knee crossed over the other as usual, the empty glass of lemonade on the table next to him replaced by a tumbler of whiskey. I walked up the steps. "Mom drinks wine when things get rough."

"I'm not your mother."

Ouch. He was pissed. I hesitated, wondering if I should just go inside, but then sat down next to him, staring out at the same neighborhood. I'm sure we saw different things. "I'm not going to apologize."

"Then don't, Poe."

"Well, I'm not."

"I'm not asking you to."

"Why not?"

Moments passed, and he took a sip of his drink. "Poe, there's a difference between . . ." He turned his face toward me, the sun catching it through the branches of the maple tree. "There's a difference between fighting for something you believe in and fighting against something you simply want to destroy."

"What does that mean?"

"It means that if your intention was to humiliate Mr. Halvorson and me today, you succeeded."

"I just said the truth. If you can't take it, that's your problem."

"No, Poe, it's not my problem, and that's what you don't understand. You want to change what happens at school, and whether you like it or not, you can't do that without making the school believe in you. You didn't do that today." He paused. "You didn't show me you were right today, Poe. You showed me how much contempt you have for me and what I believe in."

"So you're mad."

"Yes, I am. But it doesn't matter if I am. It matters that you understand what I just explained. You are right, Poe. Benders High needs change." He paused. "You have a good heart, you care about your friend, and you have that same desire in you as your mother to make things right. But if you allow your contempt for others to control it, you'll drive everything you care about away. You'll be alone, Poe, and you'll fail."

I sat there thinking. I was right. They were wrong. But I knew my dad wasn't talking about Benders High School. He was talking about us. About us all those years ago when I was a baby. "So basically what you're saying is that you ran away because Mom does what I do. She fucks every-thing up." I smirked. "At least she was there. What's your excuse?"

The sprinklers on the lawn across the street popped up and began sprinkling, covering the emerald green in a haze of sparkling mist. He cleared his throat. "I don't have one."

The tone of his voice made the world stop for me. I looked over at him, and he sat there staring at those sprinklers like a stone-skinned liar with the truth buried so deep inside nothing would let it out. I stood. "I've got to go."

"Where are you going?"

"I don't know. Out. I need to think."

Chapter Twenty-five

I walked and eventually wound my way around town, gravitat-ing toward Theo's house. I knocked, and Mr. Dorr answered. He smiled, shaking my hand. "Poe. I suppose you're here to sign on to my next reelection campaign? We're always in need of volunteers, and if I'm to crush the opposition, we need fighters on our side."

"Um, no."

"Oh. Well, then, you might want to see my son?"

"Yes."

He stepped aside, sweeping his arm inside. "Come in." He turned. "THEO!" he bellowed, rattling my eardrums. "POE IS HERE!" He turned back to me, the expression on his face not giving away that he'd just yelled loud enough to shake the windows. "Theo tells me you're giving everybody hell."

I looked around, then met his eyes. "Yes."

His eyes twinkled. "I've never known a person with a Mohawk." He patted his thick and black hair. "Think I could pull it off?"

I smiled. "Not really."

"Damn. Everybody is so stuffy around here." He smiled back. "Especially those choir people."

I laughed. "Theo has talked to you, I take it?"

He nodded. "When your son speaks in metaphorical phrases constantly, sometimes it's difficult to discern what happened, but yes, I got the picture."

Just then, Theo came up the stairs. "Dad, leave her alone."

Mr. Dorr glanced at Theo. "The prince has arrived. Good luck, Poe." Then he was off and sauntering down the hall. Theo smiled, pecking me on the lips. "What're you doing here?"

"Out for a walk."

"So you got in a fight with your dad?" He smiled.

I rolled my eyes. "Yeah. No. It was weird. Can I use your phone?"

He nodded. "Sure. I was downstairs in the music room. Come on."

Once in the room, Theo grabbed his cell and handed it to me, then sat behind his drum set. "So what's up?"

"I need to call somebody."

He looked at the phone, giving me a cockeyed look. "Sort of figured that out when you asked to use my phone."

"I'll pay you for it."

He shrugged. "Money grows on trees around here. Don't sweat it."

"South America?"

He laughed. "A kiss for each minute. Deal?"

I smiled. "Sure."

"Want me to leave?"

"Please."

He got up, touching my shoulder as he walked by. "I'll

be outside the door trying to hear what you say. Just come out when you're done."

I rolled my eyes. "Jerk."

"Love you too, honey. Good luck." Then he was gone, shutting the door behind him.

I dialed. She answered after four rings. "Dr. Holly speaking."

"Why did Dad leave?"

"What? Poe? What's going on? Are you all right?"

"Why did Dad leave?" I repeated.

"Poe, listen, this is certainly not the time to talk about . . ."

"Tell me the truth. Why did he leave?"

Her voice lowered, anger brimming to the surface. "What did he say, Poe? What is happening?"

"He didn't say anything, and that's the problem. Neither of you will. So tell me. What did you do?"

"Let me talk to him this instant. Now."

"No."

"Why he and I divorced is none of your business, young lady."

Tears welled in my eyes. "You can't even say his name, can you? It's David, and *he* is my father, and it is my business because I'm part of this family. So tell me why you never even showed me a picture of him. Tell me, Mom."

The line crackled, and her tone softened. "Poe, I'd really like to talk about this in person. Let's not get into this now."

"You drove him away, didn't you? You did the same thing to him that you do to me, and now I'm doing it to everybody around me, so tell me."

"I've told you before, Poe. Your father and I took different paths. We—"

"TELL ME!" I screamed, frightened at how much I sounded like her. "You didn't take different paths! You made it so bad for him he had to leave, didn't you? You hurt him, didn't you? DIDN'T YOU!!!"

This time her voice cracked instead of the line. "Poe, please. Calm down."

Tears streamed down my face. What was I? What was happening? Why couldn't I just be normal? Why couldn't anything work in my life? Why was this rage in me? I sniffed. "You're a liar. You're all stinking liars, and I hate you. I hate you all. You ruin my life and leave me and send me here to live with a man you hate, and you expect me to calm down? Fuck you, Mom. I hate you."

Silence.

I wiped my nose. "I've got to go. Bye."

"No. Don't hang up. Please."

I didn't hang up.

A minute passed. "Are you there?"

I swallowed. "Yes."

"Poe, I loved your father. He's a compassionate and gentle human being, and I did hurt him. I resented his weaknesses and showed him my contempt when he needed help, and I did end up hating him. I hated him for being afraid, because I was afraid. We were so young. We were pursuing our careers and our dreams, and it just became too much. I was in school, your father was devoted to writing, and I left it to him."

"Left what to him?"

A long moment passed. "You."

199

"What?"

"I was in medical school, Poe. Gone all the time, and the pressure was tremendous. And when I realized he was sacrificing his dream for you, I hated him even more, because I wasn't willing to do it."

My mind roiled, remembering all the nannies I'd had growing up. "What did you do to him?"

"I found somebody else."

My stomach sank. "He caught you, didn't he?"

Her voice faltered. "Yes."

I stood there, stunned. This wasn't supposed to happen. Not with my mom. Not with this man who was my father. My mother had been immune to life's failures forever. She was the most moralistic tightwad I'd ever known. And she'd cheated. All of a sudden, I didn't want the truth anymore. I didn't want to hear her say she was human. She'd never been human. My dad's words ran through me about contempt. About being alone. I realized my mother had always been alone. She never let anybody in, and her contempt kept everybody out. It even kept me out.

"Are you there, Poe?"

"So he left."

"No. I told him to go."

"And he came here and hid."

"Maybe so. I don't know."

The acid on my tongue burnt. I had to spit it out. "So now you pretend you're good, huh? Better than everybody else? That's why?"

"Poe, that's not fair, and it's not true. I hurt your father, I'm sure I hurt him horribly, but I've come to terms with it, and I hope that he has, too. If he hasn't, though,

I can't be held responsible." She paused. "What is he telling you?"

"Not this."

"Poe, please. You've got to understand. It was an affair. We were impetuous and immature, and things like that happen."

I took a breath, trying to bend my mind around what she was saying. "You know what, Mom? I know how he feels. I know what it feels like to have my own mom care about her stinking patients more than me. I hope South America was worth it." Then I hung up. I raised my voice to Theo, who I knew was right outside. "You can come in now."

The door opened, and Theo came in, open-faced and unashamed for listening in. "Wow. You okay?"

I handed him his phone, then slouched on the stool in front of the microphone. "I guess I didn't want to know why he left."

"What happened?"

"She cheated on him. And she didn't want to take care of me when I was little." I tapped the microphone with my finger, thinking. "She was in medical school." I rolled my eyes. "That's always been more important. I remember my nannies more than her."

"People cheat on people all the time, Poe. She's still your mom."

"No, Theo, you don't understand. I can't even get a break for stealing a cookie without an hour-long diatribe about how bad I am, but she can go screw some guy while my dad is home taking care of me. That's uncool." I shook my head. "She won't let anything go, you know? She expects everybody around her to be perfect, and when they're not, she goes on a rampage. She has like zero tolerance for everybody."

Theo laughed. "Sounds like somebody I know."

"Thanks. That makes me feel much better."

He shrugged. "You feel better knowing you're just like your mom?"

"It's called sarcasm, dummy."

"I know, but I'm serious."

"I'd never do that to my dad." I looked at him. "Or you."

He furrowed his brow, incredulous. "I've seen you in action, Poe."

"What does that mean?"

He smiled. "Uh, like today? You ripped your dad a new asshole in that room."

I looked away. "I've spent my whole life trying to not be like her."

"So raging against your dad and embarrassing the shit out of him in front of all the dorks of the school who rely on him isn't being like her?"

I remembered all the times my mom would storm into the school office and ream everybody when she had a problem. I also remembered wishing I didn't know her. It was embarrassing. "I don't need this from you right now, Theo."

He looked away. "Listen, Poe. You're upset. I would be upset, too. But you know what? You walk around acting like you're the only one dealing with crap, but you're not." He stopped, searching my face.

"You have no right to judge."

He smirked, unforgiving. He simply wouldn't feel sorry for me. "Come on. You know that's the biggest lump of politically correct horse crap there is. I do judge you. And your mom. And your dad. And everybody. We all do." He exhaled, frustrated, knowing I was mad at him. "Listen. Your mom was wrong to do what she did and your dad was wrong to roll over and walk out of your life and the school is wrong and so is Colby Morris and so is Velveeta for getting back at him with the car-bashing thing. But you know what that means? It means the world is never going to be perfect for you, and if you expect to force it to be, you're wrong, too."

"So then I should just not care?"

"If that's what floats your boat, sure." He laughed. "You know what my dad hates more than meat loaf?"

"What?"

"Politicians."

"Then why is he one?"

He nodded. "Exactly my point."

Chapter Twenty-six

The question played over and over in my mind as I walked home, and I couldn't come up with anything. What should I do? I wished I could separate all the things going on in my life, but I couldn't. My mom and her way of leaving a path of destruction behind her when the world wasn't right, my dad either running away or just going with the flow of everything.

Then there was Velveeta, his busted-up face, and how far Colby might go. The stinking school and their rules, I thought. How could my dad be a part of something so wrong? How could I try to do something right and have everything go so wrong?

Everything whirled through me like a plague of locusts, eating me alive from a thousand different places. I felt like running. I wanted to just go away, but I didn't have any-where to go. I couldn't crawl from my skin and be some-body else.

If this was growing up, I didn't want to. They could take this world and stuff it. Then I thought about Theo's dad. The politician. The man who hated what he was. The guy who played the game to change the game. I wanted to think my dad was that way, but he wasn't. Not really. He didn't stand for much of anything. He never had.

The entryway light was on when I got home, but otherwise, all was dark. I padded to Dad's study, saw light coming from underneath the door, and knocked. "Come in."

He sat behind his computer, the glow from the screen casting his face in opaque light, and he nodded. I stepped inside. "Hi."

"Hi."

"Busy?"

"No. What's on your mind?"

I studied his face for a moment. "She called you, didn't she?"

He nodded.

"Was she pissed?"

"No. We talked."

The silence in the room was cut by the fan on his computer kicking on. My mom couldn't "talk" about anything. And I knew my dad well enough that he'd just sit there and listen to what the master plan would be. The lamp and the dictator. It made me sick. And I also knew that just like everything else in his life, when my mom got home, he'd just let me go again. See ya, Poe.

They were a pair, all right. I looked at him in the dim light, and Velveeta came to my mind. My dad and his school were doing the same thing to Vel that he'd done to me. Just walk away from it. Ignore it with pretty and soothing words that don't mean a fucking thing. I had nothing to say to him, and as I turned away, he cleared his throat. "You okay, Poe?"

I turned back. "No."

Chapter Twenty-seven

"I need to see Detective Worthy, please."

The woman behind the counter looked at me, took in the Mohawk, furrowed her brow, and nodded. "Just one moment. I'll see if he's in."

I took a breath, looking around the school district offices where the detective worked from, then sat in a waiting chair next to the coffee machine. The woman picked up the phone, pushed a button, spoke a few words, then hung up. She looked at me. "He'll be out shortly." She didn't look away. "Shouldn't you be in school?"

"Yes," I said, the irony of sitting in the district office while I skipped school not lost on me. Sort of like a wanted criminal hanging out at the police station.

She stared, waiting for an explanation of why I would be skipping school, and when she didn't get one, she frowned and went back to whatever work a person like her did.

Detective Worthy came out a few minutes later. He was wearing the same tie as the day he'd told me nothing could be done about Colby Morris. He stopped short, looking at me. "Ms. Holly"—he nodded—"follow me."

I did, and he wound his way back through cubicles, finally coming to an office with his name on the door. He opened it, gesturing me inside. He strode past me, taking a seat behind his desk. I sat in one of the two chairs facing him. The look in his eyes told me there was no love lost. He didn't like me, and I didn't blame him, but I also knew that any apology I gave him wouldn't matter. Detective Worthy was just like Mom. Prove it, don't say it.

He leaned forward, steepling his fingers on the desk. "What can I do for you?"

"I'm here about Colby Morris."

His eyes hardened. "Ms. Holly, I've already told you—"

I shook my head. "I understand, Detective. And I'm not here to argue with you, either."

"Then what do you want?"

I took the surveillance records of Colby and Velveeta being in the bathroom at the same time, and I set them on his desk. "These records prove that Colby Morris, along with half the football team, was in the bathroom when Velveeta was beaten."

He didn't even look at them. "I'm aware of those records, Ms. Holly, and have looked at them. But unfortunately, it only proves that his ID card was in there. Not him. And even if he was in there, I can't prove he was the perpetrator."

"I know. And I also know that if Velveeta had been the one beating the heck out of Colby, somehow people in this town, especially Colby's dad, would see these records differently."

He sat back, crossing his arms. "The law is the law, Ms. Holly."

I thought of my dad. *I'm trying, here. I am.* I swallowed my anger, taking a moment, then thought about Theo's dad playing the game. I finally understood. I had to find out where this guy stood. Or who he stood with. Then I had to figure out what turned his crank. "What if you had evidence? Would Colby's dad order you to shut up about that, too?"

His eyes flared, and his jaw set. "Colby's father doesn't pull my strings. Nobody does."

I had my answer. The flash in his eyes told me volumes. I would have bet my South American–loving mother that it even went beyond my questioning his integrity. This guy *didn't like Colby's dad.* I backed off. "I know. And I'm not blaming you. It's just frustrating." I paused. "Other than Velveeta telling you who did it, what would work?"

He smiled. "If Colby Morris walked in here and confessed, the district attorney would be hard-pressed to ignore it."

"But that's not going to happen, right?"

He chuckled. "Don't hold your breath."

"Colby is after him again."

"I'm aware of the rumors."

That surprised me. He was sharp. "You know what people do when they think they're untouchable, Detective?"

He took a moment. "Yes, I do, Poe."

I nodded. "Me too."

He pulled out a business card. "Listen, Poe, I know how these things usually work. If you hear anything at all, call me." He held the card out to me.

I took it, then stood. "Okay." I tucked the card in my pocket, and as I walked from the building, I knew what I had to do.

Chapter Twenty-eight

"Heard anything?" I said.

Theo nodded. "Not a good situation," he said, walking through the student parking lot with me after school. I'd skipped the rest of the day, taking care of a few things before meeting up with him, and the town was readying itself for the Night of Stars picnic deal later.

"Why? What's happening?"

He stopped, stuffing his hands in his pockets. "It's what *isn't* happening."

"Enough with the cloak-and-dagger stuff, Theo. Tell me."

"Nobody's talking, which means trouble. Not even the team is blowing about it, and they usually can't keep their mouths shut about anything. Weird, because yesterday guys were taking bets in the cafeteria on how many bones would be broken after Colby caught up with Velveeta. Five seemed to be a favorite."

"Was Vel in class today?"

He nodded, walking on. "Yeah. But it was funny, because he seemed . . . normal. At least for somebody looking down the black chasm of death."

I shook my head. "Ever the optimist."

"Yep." A moment passed. "You are going to the gala event with me this evening, right?"

I rolled my eyes. "Do I have to?"

He smiled. "Yes. You can't leave me hanging out all by myself."

"Fine."

"Good." He stopped, looking across the parking lot. Colby Morris stood at his car with Ron Jameson, plucking a white square of paper from his newly replaced windshield. He opened it, read something, then handed it to Ron, who laughed, then gave Colby a high five. Theo smirked. "Something is going on."

I stared. "Looks like."

Chapter Twenty-nine

Twelve picnic tables lined up in a row spilled over with potluck food, and Benders High streamers fluttering from tree branches and lampposts celebrated the students who mattered in this place. I couldn't help but want to rip them down. Everybody in this town was ridiculous.

Carnival-like stands dotted the park here and there, with children getting their faces painted, fishing for plastic ducks, bobbing for apples, tossing water balloons to slamdunk teachers into a pool. Gaggles of women stood around gossiping, and groups of men with championship rings on their fingers and beers in their hands talked about games gone by and what was wrong with the world today.

At the far end of the green expanse, a stage, backlit with the setting sun, took center to the park. Several guys strung cables and set up instruments, and a woman on a microphone incessantly cackled, "Testing, testing, one, two, three." The whole scene made me want to hang myself from the nearest tree and stretch my neck. All this for less than five percent of the student body.

I walked past the tables and made my way through

the crowd, looking for Theo and keeping an eye out for Colby, and glanced at the digital bank clock across the street. Six-thirty. The one good thing about wearing a spiked Mohawk and enough eyeliner to black out New York City was that when people saw you, they generally got out of your way. I was like a cloud of noxious gas wafting through the celebration.

To the right of the stage, cars jammed the parking lot, and a few people, potluck trays in hand, moved toward the park. I spotted Colby's car at the far end of the lot, the windows replaced but dents still checkering the body. No Colby.

"Hey, girl."

I turned, hitching my backpack higher on my shoulder, and Theo stood at the parking lot curb, holding a tray of food. His father followed, balancing a tray in each hand. Mrs. Dorr was next, wearing a huge floppy summer hat and carrying matching bags full of plates and forks and napkins. I smiled at Mr. Dorr as he gave me a shamed look and passed, Mrs. Dorr hollering after him to put the trays at the right table. Her ever-present smile widened as she swept past me. "Lovely hair, Poe, lovely."

I blinked, and Theo laughed as we watched her bustle over to Mr. Dorr. "This is her main event of the year. Just don't get in the way."

I laughed, too, peeking at his Saran Wrap–covered tray. "Looks good."

He screwed his eyes up. "Salmon pâté with arugula? You're kidding, right?"

"I love salmon."

"Fish killer," he said as we walked to the table, where

Mrs. Dorr was carefully placing colored umbrella tooth-picks in each of some sort of gourmet mini-meatballs. She took the tray from him and busied herself once again, muttering about the horrendous fly problem in Benders Hollow and how something should be done about it. Mr. Dorr said he'd get somebody right on it. Theo took my hand. "Let's get out of here before she puts us on flyswatter patrol."

I glanced at the clock again. "We've got to talk."

He looked at me as I led him under a tree. We sat. He picked a blade of grass. "Sounds serious."

"It is."

"Were the umbrellas too much? The debate raged all morning."

"No."

"Oh. Serious, serious, then."

I nodded. "I need your help."

"With what?"

I told him, and his eyes widened as I did.

Chapter Thirty

"You're either going to be some kind of black sheep hero or dead. You know that, right?"

We crouched in the bushes of the vacant lot where I'd seen Colby and Ron make Velveeta eat Anna's note. "That's why you're here. To protect me. And him."

"This could go WAAAY wrong, Poe. In a seriously bad kind of way."

"Nobody else will do anything."

"What if what's his face doesn't show up?"

"He will."

"And you expect me to be able to do anything if he doesn't? I'd need a gun. Or twenty years of martial arts training."

I opened the pack, digging inside. "No. You just need this."

Chapter Thirty-one

Seven o'clock. That's what the note on Colby's windshield had said. Be there or be a loser. I knew that's what the note said, because I'd written it and stuck it under his windshield wiper. I'd made it short and vague, trying to copy Velveeta's scribbly writing.

> Jerkwad,
> Meet me at the place where you made me eat the note and I'll make you eat this one. Seven tonight. PS It was fun smashing yore windows.
> Velveeta

I knew Colby would show up. He wouldn't be able to resist the opportunity. I knew Velveeta would show up, too, because I'd left him a note written in my own hand.

> Velveeta,
> I'm leaving tomorrow. Can we talk? Meet me at the vacant lot at seven.
> Thanks,
> Poe

I felt like some sort of sadistic matchmaker from hell, but this had to work. I had to play the game. I had to end it, and

215

I had to show Benders Hollow, and Benders High School, that ignoring what was wrong didn't make it go away. I'd stuff it down their throats like my mom would, but I'd do it within the rules my dad cherished so much. Except this was dangerous. Very dangerous.

The church bell began ringing in the distance, and from my hiding spot, across the clearing from where Theo was, I heard branches move and leaves shake. Somebody was coming down the path. My breath caught, and I held it. Yes. Somebody was coming. In another moment, Velveeta appeared, stopping at the edge of the little open spot, looking around, then scratching his head. He opened the note I'd left him, reading it again, then stepped further into the clearing. I didn't move.

After a moment, Velveeta called my name. I held my breath again. He frowned, looking around, then froze, staring down the path. His jaw clenched, and in the late-afternoon light, Colby Morris appeared. Velveeta took a few steps back. Colby smiled, stepping closer. Ten yards separated them.

"So you decided to stop being a pussy and settle this, huh?" Colby said.

Velveeta stared.

Colby took the note out. "Going to make me eat it, huh?"

Velveeta stepped back again. "I don't know what . . ."

"Come on, pussy boy." Colby crumpled up the note, then threw it to the ground between them. "Make me eat it."

Velveeta was about to say something when I stepped out of my spot. Both stared. Then Colby laughed. "Looks like your little protector girl showed up. God, man, you are the biggest . . ."

"Does it make you feel good?"

Colby stopped. "What?"

"Does it make you feel good to hurt him?"

He narrowed his eyes, then grinned. "Just a bit of fun, freako. That's all."

"You put him in the hospital, Colby. Did it feel good?"

"About as good as it's going to feel to do it again."

"You do it because you know nobody will do anything, huh? Wow, what a tough guy," I said.

He smirked. "Yeah, that's about it. He doesn't belong here, and neither do you." He gestured around himself. "And everybody around here knows it." He looked at Vel. "You know it, too, don't you? You're like the scum at the bottom of the human shit barrel, man."

I cut in. "They know you were in the bathroom, Colby. They know you did it."

He sneered. "Yeah, so? But guess what? Even your little paper trail didn't do squat, did it?"

"So you can just walk into the bathroom, almost kill Velveeta, and walk away without anything happening. Awesome power, Colby," I said.

He shrugged, full of contempt. "Shit, freako, you saw me do it, and I'm standing here, right? And desert rat here didn't say a word about it, huh?" He looked at Vel. "You got my message loud and clear, didn't you?"

I frowned. "What message?"

He laughed. "What? You didn't tell her?" He looked at me. "We had a little discussion before you came into the bathroom. About you. 'Course I was kicking his fucking head in at the time, but he heard me."

I stared.

He chuckled. "Good old Velveeta cheese head here knows how to keep his mouth shut when it comes to girls he likes."

"What did you say?"

He shrugged. "I told him me and the guys would have some fun with you if he decided to have a conversation with anybody." He looked at my chest. "Sorta wish he had, you know? Not like anything would have happened to me if he had spilled his guts." He looked at Vel. "By the way. You owe me a new pair of shoes. They got stained when I was busting your face open."

Velveeta swallowed, shaking his head. "Wha . . ."

My heart raced. "So now what? You're going to kill him?"

"Naw. I am going to break his balls, though. Literally. I'm going to kick them so far up his ass he'll be a chick from now on. And that's just for messing with my car."

I swallowed. "No, you're not."

He stepped forward. "Oh yeah, I am. And you're not going to say a word about it just like your little friend here, because if you do, I'll make you wish you were dead."

"Detective Worthy is after you."

"Detective Worthy is a washed-up hack. He tried, and he'll keep trying, but one call from my dad to the DA made it clear. Ain't gonna happen."

I took a breath, calming myself. I forced a smile, shoving the fear away. The most dangerous thing about Colby Morris was that he *really* believed he could do anything. "No, it is going to happen. And your scholarship is going to go away. UCLA, right? I looked up breach of contract."

He faltered. "What?"

"If you are charged and convicted of a crime, your contract is breached. No scholarship. Not to UCLA, and not to anywhere."

He smiled, wicked and sharp. "Won't happen. Even if you did talk, it'd be my word against yours, and the DA likes me. Fact is, he played ball for Benders High."

I smiled. "He'd have to charge you if you confessed, though."

"Yeah, and there's about no chance in hell that would happen." He stepped forward, toward Velveeta. "Time to make me eat the note, rat boy."

"He didn't write it. I did."

Colby stopped.

"That's right. I wrote it. And I brought Velveeta here."

I could almost see the wheels turning in his head.

"You're an idiot, Colby," I said. "You just confessed."

He furrowed his brow.

"Theo," I called. Theo stepped out of the foliage, holding the video camera I'd taken from Dad's study earlier. He continued filming. I looked at Colby. "You're done, Colby."

Rage lit his face. Now the dangerous part. The part where timing was everything. He clenched his teeth. "Give me the tape."

Theo backed up, bracing himself. He kept the camera rolling. "Colby, she beat you. Just give it up for once, huh?" he said, backing up another step as Colby tensed. "Don't do it, man. It will only make things worse."

"I swear to God if you don't . . . ," Colby started, then lunged at Theo. He was fast. Theo wasn't, and Colby's fist crushed into his face. The camera flew from his hands, and before Theo hit the ground, another stiff roundhouse rocked the side of his head. I jumped forward, and as Colby went for the camera and Theo crumpled to the ground, I kicked. Hard. From behind, my foot caught him square in the crotch, and the air exploded from his lungs.

Colby bellowed in pain, falling to his knees in an instant, his chest heaving, guttural moans filling the clearing. Then he spun, quick as a viper, and hooked his arm behind my knees, taking me to the ground with a bone-jarring crash. Then he was on me, swinging wildly, hitting my face, pummeling my ribs. I'd never been hit so hard, and terrific pain exploded through my entire body as he let loose. He wouldn't stop, I knew. Nothing could stop him.

Blood poured from my nose and mouth and the clearing faded as the flurry continued, darkness closing in around me, my vision failing. I knew only seconds had passed, but eternity stretched itself out, and as the pain lessened, my body numb, I knew I'd be unconscious in another moment. He'd gone crazy, and this wouldn't be a beating. No. It would be a murder.

Then he was off me.

I opened my eyes to the sting of blood, and Velveeta was on him, enraged and frenzied as their bodies tangled. Punches landed and elbows gouged as they rolled on the ground, a wiry whirlwind and an adrenaline-consumed punching machine creating a sickening and ugly movie of just how fucked up the world can be.

I screamed no in my head a thousand times, my lips frozen and body paralyzed as violence rained down in the clearing like a nightmare storm. A storm I'd unleashed and a storm, I saw, that Colby Morris was drowning in. Tears sprang to my eyes as Velveeta wrapped his fingers around Colby's throat, his hands bone white as he squeezed.

I finally did scream as Colby's face turned a shade of deep purple and his body went slack, and Velveeta looked over, his eyes dark and primal as he sat atop Colby. I shook my head. "No, Vel. Not this way. Please. Stop," I croaked.

Nothing registered in his eyes.

Then a bull in a white button-up Sears work shirt charged into the clearing, crashing into both of them, thick arms yanking Velveeta from Colby.

"ENOUGH!" Detective Worthy bellowed, his chest heaving, his face contorted in anger as he drew his sidearm. Colby lay still, staring at Worthy as he gasped for air. Velveeta gazed at the gun like it was a foreign object.

Seconds passed. Theo moved. I dragged myself over to him.

Colby stared.

My face hurt as I looked at him. "You're done."

Chapter Thirty-two

I opened the door to a woman wearing tan cargo pants, a heavy cotton white button-up Levi's shirt, and boots. She'd lost a good ten or fifteen pounds, and I put it down to the South American jungle taking its toll. I looked her up and down, stunned. "What are you doing here?"

Her surprise was as great as mine as she looked at my eye, which was still black from Colby's fist. "Oh my God, Poe, what happened to you?"

"I got in a fight. What are you doing not in South America?"

Her eyes, always intense, met mine. No smile, but not a frown. Hard, but not mad, and a question in them. "I rode eighty miles in the back of a feed truck and caught the first flight I could after we talked. Is your father home?"

My heart stopped even as my breath fluttered. A herd of cockroaches stampeded in my stomach. "Yes."

She stood there for another moment, then leaned forward and hugged me. "Am I going to stand here all afternoon, or are you going to invite me in?"

Dad's voice came from behind. "Poe, who's at the . . ."

222

Silence. I stepped aside.

They stood feet apart. I was a baby the last time they'd seen each other. Neither spoke; both stared. I got the feeling the last fifteen years sped by in a matter of seconds. Then she smiled, nodding. "Hello, David."

He stepped forward. "Hello, Nancy."

I gaped. "What are you doing here, Mom?"

She looked at me, and something I'd never seen in her eyes shined like tiny diamonds floating in blue pools. Sadness. She glanced at Dad, then back to me. "I thought it would be a good time to begin repairing what should have been repaired a long time ago."

Dad stood there at the door, a man alone for so long he scrubbed grout lines with a toothbrush; then he stepped aside. "Please, come in."

Epilogue

"My name is Poe Holly, and I'm new here." I stood on the stage
of the school's acoustically perfect auditorium. My black
eye had faded. Behind me, the choir stood in their gowns,
and in front of me, hundreds of people waited patiently.
Theo waved from his seat. He'd rented a tuxedo in honor of
me. What a dork.

I saw Anna Conrad's father in the third row, her mother
sitting next to him as she scowled at me. Anna sat next to
her, grinning like a prom queen fool, and I couldn't help
but smile. Ever since she'd quit choir, her home had been
an endless and blissful hell. Endless because her mother
was unrelenting, and blissful because Anna wouldn't
change her mind. We'd actually become friends, and for being a real-life Barbie, she wasn't that bad.

It had been two weeks since my mother showed up at
the front door, and as I scanned the crowd and found her
and my dad, I gave them a small wave. They were weird.
Parents are weird. After that first tense and almost alter-
universe experience with my mom and dad sitting at the
dinner table together, they'd let me know she was staying

for a week or so to "sort things out." My dad explained that even apart, we were a family, and a family had to get to know each other to function.

No, they aren't together, and no, I don't think they ever will be, and yes, I will always have my fingers crossed that they will love each other again, but over the last little while, I'd seen changes in both of them. Maybe new changes, but seeing them live in the same house and cook the same dinners and sit at the same table to eat, I thought that maybe those changes were old, like when they'd been together before I came along.

I thought they were good for each other, but just like medicine, sometimes the worst-tasting crap is the best for you.

For every wicked outburst my mother was prone to (especially concerning how late I could stay out with Theo, my grades, the new tattoo I wanted), my dad was the placid lake of reason and diplomacy. It was like salt and pepper, I suppose. When they mixed, they mellowed each other out. My dad was much less of a lamp with her support, and the fire in her eyes was less apt to burn you to a crisp with his. She was leaving tomorrow, and I was going to actually miss her. She'd stayed an extra few days to see this, and I guess it proved something to me.

I cleared my throat, glancing to the side and catching Mrs. Baird's eye. She was cool, really, and I was learning that her choir wasn't traditional at all, which I liked because that made her brave.

My dad had pressed for a PTA meeting about the rules for tryouts, and as the debate began between us and the choir committee and the PTA, Mrs. Baird stood up, furnished a copy of tryout rules she'd written up, and told everybody that if they didn't accept them, she'd resign. End of story. She'd led five of the seven choir ensembles to state championships in the last eight years, and nobody wanted to see that go away.

I scanned the crowd, thinking of everything that had happened. Colby Morris was charged and convicted in juvenile court on four counts of assault: two for Velveeta, one for me, and one for Theo, but he didn't go to juvie. His father pulled strings and he was put on probation, but the college scouts disappeared after he tested positive during the court-mandated drug test. He'd been popping OxyContin for a year, and he was sitting in a detox center somewhere in Sacramento until he regained his sanity.

And then there was Velveeta. He's gone, back to the desert and on his own. He didn't say goodbye. I don't think he likes goodbyes. But he did leave me a note. This is what it said:

Po,
I'm going home. This place ain't for me.
Velveeta

I'll miss him, just like I miss my buds back home. This place can be brutal, but I'm staying. I've started something here, and I intend to finish it without ruining my life in doing so. Dad scrapped his book and decided to write a new one. This one is about bullying, but it's not for students. It's for the adults and schools that let it happen. In a moment of harsh honesty, he said that Velveeta might be lost, but maybe there was another kid out there who wasn't quite as lost.

So there it is, messy and untidy just like my life, and now I'm going to do what comes next. I'm going to sing, my mom is going back to South America, my dad is going to burrow himself in his study to write, and this world is going to keep going around like a wobbly wheel with a bent axle.

Oh yeah, and when I'm done singing, my dad is going to stand up, clap his hands until they're red, and say, "That's my daughter up there." And I'm going to like it.

Acknowledgments

I'd like to thank my wife, Kimberly, and my family, but not our dogs. They bug me.

Gratitude goes to my agent, George Nicholson, of Sterling Lord Literistic, for yet again defying the odds. To my editor, Joan Slattery, and Allison Wortche, assistant editor, thank you for your attention and outstanding guidance.

There is a place where a river runs through it. I will be there.

　　　　　　　　　　　　　　　　　　　　　　　　—Anon.

Michael Harmon is the author of *The Last Exit to Normal,* which *School Library Journal* hailed as "an excellent read" in a starred review, and *Skate,* praised as a "remarkable first novel" by *Kirkus Reviews* and selected as an ALA Quick Pick. He was born in Los Angeles and now lives in the Pacific Northwest, where he enjoys woodworking, reading, fishing, backpacking, poker, steak, and really loud music.

To learn more about Michael Harmon and his books, please visit www.booksbyharmon.com.